The Green Zone

Larry Skeete

iUniverse, Inc.
New York Bloomington

The Green Zone

Copyright © 2009 by Larry Skeete

This is a work of fiction. All of the characters, names, incidents, organizations, and dialogue in this novel are either the products of the author's imagination or are used fictitiously.

iUniverse books may be ordered through booksellers or by contacting:

iUniverse
1663 Liberty Drive
Bloomington, IN 47403
www.iuniverse.com
1-800-Authors (1-800-288-4677)

ISBN: 978-1-4401-3889-8 (pbk)
ISBN: 978-1-4401-3890-4 (ebk)

Printed in the United States of America

iUniverse rev. date: 4/11/2009

Character Biographies

Neil Burke: Director of Terrorism Analysis at the Department of Homeland Security

Marwan Barghouti: Hezbollah Operative

Janet Kilpatrick: Weather reporter WSNO Chicago

Bob Gordon: Assistant Director of Terrorism Analysis

General Frank Beamer: CENTCOM Commander

Larry Rivers: Producer WSNO Chicago

Gerald Clark: Director of Homeland Security

VJ Patel : Secretary of Defense

Chapter 1

In five minutes, it would all be over. The months of hard work, the hours spent deciphering codes, the mind numbing surveillance would all come to end. For Neil Burke however that would just mean he could turn his full attention to the next threat, but that would be then and this was now. Now meant he was in the driver's seat of a black Department of Homeland Security Crown Victoria with heavily tinted windows, waiting for the FBI agents to do their thing. He was there to make sure they followed the letter of the law and didn't give his suspect a chance to plead out later on the grounds that his rights were violated. Officially of course, he didn't have to be there, the Bureau guys were pros and knew their stuff. Even so, he could always have sent somebody else to baby-sit them. But that was not the way that Neil Burke did things. If you wanted things done properly you had to do them yourself. That was his motto. That was why he was sitting in his car, outside of a busy Starbucks on Angel Street in Providence, observing a perfectly routine FBI raid.

Their suspect was a student at Brown University who held down a part time job as a barista at Starbucks. He was a graduate student on a student visa pursuing a Ph.D. in computer engineering. That much was true, but Mr. Xi Chen was also in the employ of the interior ministry police in China. He was a high-ranking member of the communist party and adept at acquiring proprietary software and trade secrets and passing them to his bosses back in Beijing. He of course had not included this nugget of background information in his application to Brown. Everyone knows about silicone valley in California. It's the software and technology capital of the world but running a close second in terms of start-up's and sheer volume of venture capital invested is the I-95 corridor running from Boston, through Quincy and down to Providence. There are six Ivy league colleges within a 100 mile radius of Providence and thousands of newly minted graduates all dreaming of becoming the next Bill Gates or Peter Wang. Mr. Chen started off as a typical graduate student in Brown's prestigious Ph.D. computer engineering department and like most students moonlighted at some of the startups in the area. On the weekends he would grind out some laborious code and trouble shoot various programs that no one else wanted to do. The companies were happy to have this large pool of cheap talent to use and the grad students were happy to make the forty bucks an hour offered.

Xi slowly enough but over the past few months his thefts became almost brazen as his confidence grew. A manager at the software company he worked for became suspicious when he noticed several of their manuals out of place and not in order. A software company guards its basic code manuals the same way that Coke and Pepsi guard the recipe for their softdrinks, so anything out of the ordinary gets their full attention. A private security company was called in and installed a state of the art closed-circuit monitoring system and then a week later at precisely 11:23pm, Mr. Chen was seen picking the lock to the room housing the company's mainframe computer, then busily copying dozens of files to his thumb drive.

Finding a foreign national spy operating on US soil is a big deal even if the secrets they are stealing and passing on are not security related. The FBI was called and Neil was tapped to head the entire operation from Homeland Security.

The next couple of months had been spent following and observing Xi Chen and figuring out who his handlers were, and now the time had come to bring him. The plan was to take him up to the FBI field office in Boston for what was euphemistically called aggressive questioning. Eventually he would be moved to a federal detention facility in Arizona and then they would have to give the Chinese Embassy access to their citizen, but by then Mr. Chen would be hungry, sleepless, disoriented and talkative.

Neil checked his watch and wondered what was taking them so long. Three agents wearing their navy blue FBI windbreakers had gone inside two minutes ago, plenty of time to locate their guy and bring him out. Neil shifted his weight in the car and undid his seatbelt to stretch. He stifled a yawn and settled back in to his seat to wait. Suddenly the door to the Starbucks flew open and out came Xi Chen in full flight and at full speed. The three agents, looking somewhat worse for wear and followed him out into the street. Chen paused for a second, looked directly at Neil's car and then took off down the sidewalk dodging in and out of pedestrians.

"What the hell" muttered Neil.

He was parked just across the street but the car was facing the wrong direction. He started the Crown Vic, gunned the engine and did a quick fishtailing U-turn. The big car, tires squealing and engine howling took off down the street after Chen, who had already reached the end of the block. Arms churning and legs pumping, Chen was moving through the mid morning pedestrian traffic quite efficiently. He took a right at the end of the second block and started up the wrong way on one of the many narrow one-way roads that surrounded Brown. Neil brought his car to a screeching halt at the intersection, took a deep breath, rolled his shoulders and prepared to pursue Chen on foot. He removed his jacket and tie, laid it on the seat next to him ,flexed and relaxed his calves and glutes then got out. By this time Chen had a three block lead but Neil knew the area well and as he began running he focused on achieving what he thought would be a good eight hundred meter pace. With long graceful strides he brought himself up to speed and soon matched Chen's pace and was even pulling him in a little. The street they were on was a narrow one way avenue. Large oaks and pines lined the sidewalks and cast pleasant shadows. The houses were typical two storey structures, rented out on a semester basis by Brown students. It was a beautiful day, unseasonably warm and lots of the students were out in their yards catching some sun. They looked up with bemusement as first Chen and then Neil flashed by. Chen still in full stride, looked back at Neil and was surprised to find him only a block behind. Neil had put in a little extra kick and was focused on his breathing and form. His upper body was perfectly still, back erect and shoulders relaxed.

When the FBI agents came in to arrest him, Chen initially agreed to go quietly but as the lead agent approached him to put on the handcuffs, Chen struck with surprising fury. He was a trained martial artist and with a quick spin he landed a back-fist to the agents left temple dropping him to the ground. Before the other two could move he kicked the first one in the groin and then delivered an elbow to the sternum of the last agent. He had then ripped off his dark green Starbucks smock and taken off running through the door.

Chen glanced back again and Neil could see his eyes widen with shock and surprise. He was now only fifteen yards behind and appeared as relaxed as if he were out for a morning run. The three FBI men were specks in the background; the beating Chen had inflicted on them was taking its toll.

Neil noticed his quarry's form was deteriorating and gave another little kick. He would be within contact distance in about ten strides. Chen's breathing grew increasingly ragged. They had been going at full speed now for two minutes. Neil figured that Chen would have to make his play soon, while he still had enough energy to fight. The man was really laboring now and it was clear he would soon collapse from sheer exhaustion. He maneuvered over to the right of the sidewalk, put in a burst of speed and quietly pulled even. Chen's move came a fraction of a second too late. Chen stopped and whirled to his left, fists cocked and legs braced, ready to deliver a roundhouse kick to Neil's jaw. To his amazement he saw nothing. He sensed rather than saw Neil over his right shoulder. He managed to duck away from the gentle right jab that Neil threw, but was unprepared for the vicious leg kick that Neil unleashed into his left hamstring. Chen's legs buckled involuntarily, bringing his head into perfect alignment to take the full brunt of Neil's knee strike to the chin. His jaws clicked shut and the lights went out. Neil pulled out his handkerchief, he always carried one, and wiped away the moisture from his forehead, he took a few deep breaths and then placed his handcuffs on Chen's hands.

"If you want anything done right you have to do it yourself" he said, and sat down to wait for the FBI agents to catch up.

A month earlier at Miami International Airport

Thank God its almost over thought Gabriel. Ten hours of standing on your feet and dealing with a bunch of clueless tourists was enough to make anyone crazy. Their shifts were supposed to be only six hours but since the Department of Homeland Security had downsized, their supervisor had been forced to have everyone work ten hour days, What had been a nice, plush government job had become a royal pain in the ass. To make it worse he had been moved from the domestic counter to international meaning he had to deal with these non-English speaking jackasses all day long. Half of them smelled funny and the other half seemed genuinely surprised that they would have to show their passports to an immigration officer. He only had another five minutes to go; the guy in the black sweater would be his last one for the day and then he could get the hell out of here and get a beer.

"Good evening Sir. Passport please"

To his pleasant surprise the man quickly produced his passport. It was a distinctive purple color and Gabriel immediately recognized it as German. It was already opened to the visa page and showed a stamped tourist visa.

"Where are you coming from" asked Gabriel

"I'm from Hamburg but I just came in from Jamaica." replied the man with a toothy smile.

Thankfully he also spoke good English so they wouldn't have to struggle through with signs and gestures.

"What's bringing you to the US sir?"

"I came to visit some friends in Chicago. We met in graduate School."

"Okay Mr. ahhh" Gabriel paused and flipped to the front of the passport. "Mr. Tomas Erdogan how long are you planning to stay in the US?"

"It's going to be a quick trip. Just one week"

Gabriel quickly scanned the passports magnetic strip and looked up at this computer screen, The picture, name and visa all matched up. This guy was good to go and that means I'm good to go too he thought.

"Thank you Sir, welcome to the United States. Enjoy your stay"

"Oh I'm sure I will" said Marwan,

He took his passport and walked through the swing doors into the lobby. The relaxed toothy smile was gone replaced with a look of cold determination. So far so good he thought, the first hurdle had been cleared and he could now get to work.

Chapter 2

Five months later: Saturday 4:30pm Mclean Virginia.

General Richard Maldonado was enjoying the perks of post-military life. After 25 years in the Army he had started to wonder what it was like to be a regular citizen again. Twenty-five years of habit and discipline were hard to give up but he was thankful for some of the things that he could now start to take for granted. He was finally able to travel in relative anonymity, he could go for a run without two aides shadowing him, and there was never anyone waiting for him when he woke up besides his wife. Being a four star Army General had its moments but toward the end of his tenure, the security arrangements and lack of privacy had made him look forward to a return to civilian life. Recently he had been invited to sit on the boards of numerous corporations and he was starting a career as a public speaker.

"Honey have you seen my briefcase?" he asked. "I'm going to be late"

"First of all dear, you're not late, you're just not early, and your briefcase is where it always is." His wife Grace replied.

"The kitchen table?" he queried.

"No dear..its in the study on your desk" Grace Maldonado was a striking woman in every sense of the word. She graduated top of her class at Baylor Law and after marrying Richard and giving birth to their daughter, she had surprised everyone and continued her law career. Even after Richard was given the CENTCOM command she had continued to work and was now a senior partner in her firm.

Richard grabbed his briefcase and walked into the kitchen and gave Grace a hug.

"Don't forget to watch me on TV" he said.

"Of course I won't forget, silly. You just stay calm and don't get flustered and it'll be fine."

Maldonado smiled and headed out the door into the chilly evening. At this time the capital would be emptying out and traffic would be a nightmare so he was taking the train in to the city. After years of being chauffeured around he had become somewhat loath to driving himself. He was on his way into Washington to do a live interview with Jim Greyson. It would be broadcast around the country on the STAR news network and would give him the chance to talk up John Farnum. John had been one of his best pilots and a highly rated squdreon leader back in Iraq. He had an easy going charisma that made him a natural politician and it was no secret that he was eyeing the Virginia Senate seat in next years elections. They had talked last night when John had called him from London and had told him he was going to retire from American Airlines and devote himself to full time campaigning. Maldonado felt that John would be a shoo-in. He had handled himself well in the spotlight when he came back stateside as the most decorated pilot of the Iraq war. He smiled and said all the right things and had an air of confidence and competence around him.

After a ten minute walk he arrived at the train station and boarded his train just as it was about to leave the station, a couple of other commuters got on with him and he settled in for the forty-five minute ride into DC. On the way in he thought about what to expect during the interview. Jim Greyson had established himself as one of the most popular conservative talk show hosts in the country. He asked probing and insightful questions and was relentless when it came to pressing to his point of view. This interview was a follow up to an earlier one he had done during the first days of the Iraq war. This time, the shows producers had asked him to come in and talk about how he was adjusting to life as a civilian. Maldonado knew however that after a few softball questions on his wife and what it felt like to buy groceries that he would be grilled about what he thought of his CENTCOM replacement and the Secretary of Defense. That was fine he thought, he could allow himself a little latitude and give them a few sound bites and then work John Farnum into the conversation. He was a skilled speaker and felt confident that in a verbal joust he could more than hold his own. The train rattled its way slowly through the suburbs and after going through a tunnel emerged into Union station.

5:30pm Department of Homeland Security , Langley Virginia

Neil Burke was going to have to make a decision soon and he knew it. It was already late in the afternoon and was going to miss yet another run, but recent events had kept everyone working overtime. Over the past days there had been a vast upswing in the volume of data coming in from their contacts in Syria and Yemen. Something was cooking and he couldn't afford to sit on it any longer. His boss, Gerald Clark would have to be brought into the loop.

Neil's official title at the Department of Homeland Security was Director of the Office of Terrorism Analysis. In short he headed up the division that received and analyzed perceived terrorist threats. It placed him one step short of being fully in charge but his bosses' job was not something that Neil coveted. He was happy to remain anonymous as long as it allowed him to make difficult recommendations without having to worry about the political fallout they might cause. Nine years ago he had been ready to retire and go back to Cal-tech, join a think tank and do some teaching. The CIA had become moribund in red tape and bureaucracy but things changed dramatically after 9/11 and he emerged from that period recommitted and energized. The previous President had formed the DHS and for all of its faults the good news was that all the players were now under one roof. The DHS with the help of the Department of Defense was in the business of listening and observing. With hundreds of satellites in orbit and secret access to most of the electronic data stored in the world, the problem was not in obtaining data but deciding which data to analyze and review. Over the past few years with they had been able to develop a list of suspected high level terrorists throughout the world and now his job was to keep tabs on what they said and what it meant. On a typical day his office received dozens of pages of emails, chat room transcripts and intercepted phone conversations. His team would translate the material and then attempt to analyze this in real time to see if they could spot a link between what was said and what actually happened in Baghdad, Damascus and elsewhere.

The problem was that in the past days they had received not dozens but hundreds of pages per day. These guys were talking a whole lot more and that was never good, but that was not what really worried him. What had gotten his attention was the type of language they were using. On a normal day, a chat-room conversation would focus on religious holidays that were coming up, the latest news out of the Middle East or some vague ranting about the US. Very straightforward stuff without any obvious encoding or hidden messages. The last few days however the content had changed dramatically. There were lots of messages consisting only of direct quotations from the Koran, followed by seemingly unrelated quotes from the Bible. The tempo had changed considerably and the players were now communicating exclusively in some kind of coded language. He suspected that the Koranic passages were instructions identifying and alerting various team members to begin an operation and the Biblical passages were meant to identify a western target or location. That was the best his guys had been able to come up with so far and it was enough to make Neil very nervous.

Bob Gordon who was his second in command knocked on his door and then walked into the office with a grim look on his face. Bob was a runner and was lean to the point of being gaunt. He was approaching 50 but still competed in 3 triathlons a year. He was always up for a challenge and Neil depended on him for advice and to gauge the political waters.

"I think we've missed the boat on this one."

He handed Neil a thin sheaf of papers. It was dated 1/11, today's date.

"That's the latest set of translations we have" said Bob "It's a cell phone call from about twenty minutes ago"

Neil put on his glasses and began to read:

A: Well its been a while since we talked. How are you?

B: I am good. My brother is coming to visit next week and is bringing my first nephew for me to see.

A: Ah congratulations then, you must be pleased. Your brother is now finally a man.

B: Yes he is. I worried about him for a while, he was too much interested in school and not enough in his wife. (laughter)

A: What did he name the child?

B: The bastard won't tell me. He says it is a surprise.

"Are the recent intercepts all like this?" Neil asked.

Bob nodded glumly and said, "We noticed the change about 2 hours ago".

"This either means they are operational or there's been a setback and whatever they had planned was called off" said Neil.

After a few days of intense coding and a dramatic increase in the level of activity, a sudden change back to normal conversation concerned Neil more than ever. If Al-Qaeda had been planning an attack it usually went through 4 stages. First of all a long planning phase where the details of the attack were planned, agents trained and financing obtained. The second phase was immediately before the strike teams were given the green light. There would be a brief flurry of messaging back and forth with final instructions given and any adjustments made. The third stage was the operational stage which commenced immediately after an Al-Qaeda commander gave the "go" order. From that point on, until the mission was completed, the teams were on their own and there was no further communication. The fourth stage was claiming responsibility, and a brief video of the attackers would be released usually with a high level commander praising his bravery.

Neil now feared that they had just witnessed the transformation from the second to third stages and that whatever had been planned was now being carried out. He couldn't afford to wait any longer, he was going to have to notify the Director and advise an immediate upgrade of the National Threat Level to level red, the highest level. Most people would see no change in their day to day lives, but significant changes would happen behind the scenes. If the President went ahead and ordered a level red threat alert, the National Guard and Air Force would immediately scramble fighter planes for round the clock air patrols of the ten largest cities and the Capital. All of the strategic nuclear submarines that were in port would put out to sea for indefinite patrol duty. Police and firefighter leaves were effectively cancelled throughout the country and strategic sites such as bridges, utilities and dams were placed under a 24-hour watch. The President and Vice-President would be separated and remain separated in order to preserve a chain of command should they be targeted. It was not a trivial thing and Neil knew this as he reached for the phone. The only threat level higher than Red was a Code grey which signaled that the country was at war and under attack

"Maggie, I need you to page the Director to my office please". Neil looked up at Bob and said "I'm going to recommend a code red"

"I figured you would. I completely agree Neil, I don't think we have a choice the way this thing is lining up" said Bob.

"He's going to have a tough time selling this one" said Bob.

"Why is that" asked Neil but he already knew the answer.

"After the Iran fiasco we got burned pretty badly and the Director took a lot of heat for that one"

Bob was referring to the only other time the National Threat Level had been raised to lever red. A year and a half ago, a covert operation had been approved and launched against Iran. At the time the Iranians were very publicly in the process of going after a nuclear weapon. They had started processing weapons grade Uranium, built a high quality centrifuge and had brought a heavy water facility on line. From what the guys at Shin Bet, the Israeli version of the CIA had told them, it would be 6 months at best before the Iranians had enough fissile material to prepare one or two warheads. A direct strike had been ruled out as too messy, so instead a sabotage operation had been planned and carried out with spectacular results. The facilities at Natanz and Fasa were both burnt to the ground in mysterious chemical fires. The computer files and backup data storage facilities had also been wiped out and several of the key engineers had suffered mysterious accidents. The setback was by all reports catastrophic and it would take decades before they would be a threat again. The Iranian response however had been somewhat mystifying, instead of blaming the US and threatening retaliation, Tehran had simply quietly issued a statement saying that there had been a fire at one of their research labs and they were putting their quest for nuclear power on the back burner to focus on stabilizing the region. Despite the lack of a direct threat to the US, the DHS had recommended and gotten a level red alert. Congressman and Senators from both sides of the aisle immediately and publicly questioned this, demanding to know what was going on and why the country was being placed on heightened alert. The White House had remained silent on the matter and the Secretary for Homeland Defense had been forced to dredge up some old intelligence that had cleared a long time ago and use this as the public reason for the alert. It had gone over very badly in the press and the President had not been amused, but agreed that there was no other choice.

The phone rang at Neil's desk and he picked it up immediately.

"It's the Director" said Maggie.

" Gerald its Neil here, we've been watching a situation for the past few days and I think we're seeing a significant threat develop"

"What do you have" snapped Gerald. He was not a patient man.

"We've been tracking a serious upswing in coding and frequency of messages between Al-Qaeda and Hezbollah principals the past 2 days and now we're seeing a reversion back to the usual inconsequential stuff. I think we have to assume that they've gone operational. I'm recommending a full upgrade to a level red"

There was a long silence at the other end and Neil looked up at Bob and narrowed his eyes. He knew better than to speak up and knew the only thing to do was to wait until his boss had decided what to do.

"I want you in my office in 30 minutes. We're going to thrash this thing out and make a decision. If you're right we'll call the President right then and there and make our proposal. If you're wrong or just not very convincing you can explain to my grandson why I leaving his goddamned birthday party early!" the phone slammed down in Neil's ear and went dead.

5:30 pm News One Production Studio, Chicago, Illinois

So far it looked like the big news story for the night was going to be the weather. Thank God for Chicago winters thought Larry. As the evening news director at WNSO Larry Rivers had final say in what stories the station went with. On slow days like today you could always count on a good weather story to fill in the dead spots. In Chicago it was either too rainy, too cold or too windy and on the rare days when it was just perfect he would send a camera crew down to lake shore drive to shoot the bikini clad Northwestern students getting a tan. He already had a reporter on the way to O'Hare getting ready to do a live segment on the flight delays. If all went well they could get a few shots of the airport ground crew trying to clear the runways. That was always a good one he thought. He made a mental note to call Janet and remind her about that and looked at the clock on the wall; 30 minutes till show time he thought to himself.

Janet Kilpatrick had been a field reporter for the last two years at WNSO or News One as they were known in Chicago. She joined the staff as an intern straight out of college and worked her way up to live camera time in just a few years. She was a tough, hard-driving perfectionist who could be difficult to be around, but the quality of her work was never in question. So it was no surprise that the station manager had personally called her and told her to meet up with a camera crew at O'Hare. Larry her station manager and boss was famous for his last minute decisions and had decided without warning that they would lead off the news that night with live shots from the airport. She was going to need to do a two minute segment and then some "spontaneous" interaction with the anchors at the end. She'd make it look easy and would laugh and joke with the guys back in the studio about how lucky they were to be inside and then they would wrap it up and head back.

After she got the call, Janet who had been finishing up a work out at the Krav Maga center, had politely excused herself, showered and was now racing toward the airport in her BMW. The M3 wove in and out of traffic and expertly found gaps when there were none. Janet had bought the car for herself as a reward for being promoted to reporter and loved the thrill of pushing the car close to its limits. After what seemed like an eternity to her she pulled off the highway and onto a little used access road that skirted the perimeter of the airport. It had been used as a construction road during the latest runway addition but was now almost forgotten and rarely used. It was poorly maintained and had not been plowed but luckily there was a single set of tire tracks down the middle of the road and she followed these cautiously. The road looped around to the left and after a few turns she was almost at the back gate of the high school where she was to meet up with her camera crew. She had chosen this spot because it allowed for a great view of the airport and a view of the planes overhead as they came in to land. There was a dark green van already in the school parking lot and Janet immediately recognized it as belonging to her cameraman Joey. She pulled up alongside his car and got out.

"Hey Joey" she said "Looks like another weather story for us again."

The snow had stopped now and Janet went right to work rehearsing her report. It would have to look both professional but not too rehearsed. If they were lucky she would be interrupted by a plane flying overhead and she would smile sheepishly at the camera until the noise from the jet engines faded away. Live reporting was an art and she considered herself an artist of the highest order. She would allow her hair to blow into her face a few times to accentuate how windy it was and flick it out of the way. She knew that Joey liked that and it would make the rest of the evening a little more interesting. She was just getting over a break up with a lawyer and even though she would never admit it, she always enjoyed flirting with Joey. The outfit she was wearing covered her figure completely but underneath the white trench-coat was a body that demanded attention.

"Hey Janet, We're live in 2 minutes. You ready?" yelled Joey. Janet jumped a little startled out of her daydream and smiled up at her cameraman.

"Relax take it easy guy. It looks like we can get a few shots of the runway crews. They're starting to clear off one of the runways now. We might even get a landing if we're lucky." said Janet.

She ran into the van to check her makeup one last time while Joey maneuvered around to get a better look at the runway. There were a group of five snow plows making quick work of clearing the runway. Most large airports like O'Hare had heated pipes along the runways and this made it much easier to quickly clear a runway. It was more expensive but it cut the turnaround time in half after a big snowstorm.

"We're live in 30 seconds!" said Joey.

He hefted the camera onto his shoulder and began transmitting back to the studio.

Janet walked up to her mark looked into the camera and smiled.

"Good evening everyone. This is News One reporter Janet

Kilpatrick with a live report from the airport. As you can see behind me it looks like they are putting the finish touches on the runways and are getting ready to re-open O'Hare." Joey widened his shot got a quick look at the last of the plows making a final pass. The others were already parked off to the side.

"Today's snowstorm which briefly brought the nations transportation hub to a standstill dumped an estimated eight inches of snow on Chicago. Long travel delays were the norm and after two to three hour delays it looks like they are almost back in business"

Janet paused for second and sure enough she could hear the dull roar of airplane coming in overhead.

"It looks like we have our first flight coming in now. These folks have been waiting for a while to land and I'm sure they will be happy to touch down."

6:15 pm Airspace over Chicago O'Hare Airport

John Farnum was a busy man and had a lot of things on his mind. His most pressing task right now however was to clarify what he thought he had just heard from the Air Traffic controller at O'hare.

" O'Hare this is American three-niner-five. Can you repeat your previous transmission."

"American three nine five, this is O'hare, repeating. You are now clear for landing on runway 6. Please descend to three thousand feet and begin final approach."

John and his co-pilot Hank Smith looked at each other with raised eyebrows. O'Hare was telling them to go ahead and land their plane in the worst snow storm Chicago had seen in a decade. When they left Heathrow nine hours ago it had been a rare sunny winter day in London. Weather reports had called for light snow squalls in the mid west but what he was seeing now was absolute white out conditions with zero visibility. They had considered diverting to St Louis but there were reports of tornado sightings there, so here they were at 9000 feet circling in a holding pattern with 16 other jets waiting for the weather to clear.

"Uh, O'hare this is American three-niner-five again" said John, "Request continuation of current holding pattern until we get a break in the weather."

" Negative American three nine five. We are looking at a clearing weather situation within five minutes. We need you in an approach pattern at three thousand so we can get some of these other birds on the ground. Do you copy?"

"Roger O'Hare. American 395 clear". John put down the microphone , picked up the in flight intercom and said. "Folks this is your Captain from the flight deck, it looks we have some good news.....we are now cleared for landing. Once again we're sorry for the long wait but it looks like we should be on the ground in a few minutes."

John looked over at Hank and smiled, even though he didn't want to admit it, he was enjoying himself. Since leaving the Air Force for a job as a commercial pilot two years ago he had become increasingly restless with the mind-numbing predictability of his job. These big jets practically flew themselves .All he had to do was make point it in the right direction and the on board computers would do the rest. Today however there was nothing predictable about this landing. Runway 6 was the shortest of the 8 runways at O'hare but also the most sheltered and the easiest to keep snow free. The air traffic controller had picked it for this reason but it only gave John a bare 4500 feet of runway to make his landing.

John began a steep curving descent down to three thousand feet. Normally the autopilot would do this but he had just turned it off and taken manual control of the plane. His turn radius and rate of descent were significantly faster than if the Boeing had been left to its own devices, but the air traffic controller had told him they had a weather window opening up and he didn't want to miss it.

Hank glanced over as the plane rolled a few degrees past "the coffee- spill zone". He knew that John was a great pilot but all these ex-Air Force guys used the slightest excuse to take the stick. The problem was they thought they were still in Iraq trying to land in Baghdad, not bringing in a load of British tourists. Still he had to admire the dexterity with which John put the big plane through its paces. They leveled out at three thousand and Hank brought the flaps up without being told. So far so good, they were now in a direct line with the runway which was 4 miles away. With any luck they should break the cloud ceiling in a few minutes and get a visual on the runway.

John eased back into his seat and pulled the throttle back to an air speed of 220 knots. It was a little slower than he would prefer but he wanted them to hit the runway at about 180 knots instead of the usual 195. It didn't sound like much but he figured it would give them an extra few feet of stopping room. The plane shuddered and groaned, it didn't like being asked to go this slow while flying and John knew it.

"Hold on big fella, we're almost there" he murmured and edged the throttle down even more. Since leaving the Air Force 2 years ago John had quickly risen through the ranks at American to become the fastest co-pilot ever to be promoted to left chair and captain his own plane. He had been the first pilot to go through the annual 2 day flight simulator training course without an error and on nights like tonight he was proving why. In the back, the passengers glanced around nervously and shot anxious looks through the windows.

John's headset crackled with static and then burst to life "American three-nine-five, this is air traffic control, please state your location" said a new voice.

"O'Hare we are currently 2.3 miles out from runway 6, altitude 2800 feet heading vector 698". That was strange thought John, we should be on their local radar by now, but from years of flying he found it best not to question air traffic control, "Just let them do their job and I'll do mine" he thought.

Chapter 3

Neil was by nature a meticulous man and he was more than ready to defend his recommendations to Clark. As an undergraduate at Cal-tech his attention to detail had served him well and allowed him to graduate at the top of his class with dual degrees in Mathematics and Arabic languages. Among the notoriously un-physical crowd at Cal-Tech he had been the first runner in twenty years to go to Nationals, where he had placed fifth in the mile and third in the eight hundred meters. With his unique skill set the CIA had recruited him heavily and two months after graduation he had found himself at Langley in Virginia doing cryptology work. His aptitude and technical brilliance soon put him on the fast track for advancement and he had moved on to doing actual field-work for the agency in Baltimore and then Israel. That had been a dark period in his life. Just married and with a new wife back home the overseas deployment had stretched him thin. It didn't help that he had been asked to run a series of black-ops with Shin-Bet during that time. These had weighed heavily on his mind and after one particularly gruesome assassination in the Gaza strip he had returned to the agency field office and asked to be reassigned. The field director that had handled his reassignment was Gerald Clark and the two had worked together in some capacity since then.

Neil walked into the Clark's office and found him sitting impatiently at his desk waiting. Gerald Clark was a small compact man who had a brisk no nonsense approach to life. He did not suffer fools lightly and Neil knew from experience that he would have to make his case promptly and convincingly. If his analysis was poorly structured he would be picked apart and his mistakes explained in painstaking detail.

"Good evening Gerald, how are you?" said Neil.

"Get to it Neil! I didn't come here to have you enquire about my health! What do you have?". It appeared that the director was in fine form today.

"Here's some of the transcripts we started receiving Thursday night." Neil handed over a sheaf of papers. "This is from Thursday night between 9:30 and 11:55 local time. Its from a mid-level guy in Yemen and we think from voice analysis that he's talking with Sheik Abu Sitaf"

Abu-Sitaf was a fiery cleric who was the spiritual leader of a small mosque in Rome. He had been under surveillance for a few years now when his name showed up on some databases from computers captured raids in Pakistan. He was suspected of laundering money collected under the guise of an Islamic charity and then channeling it to Taliban groups in Afghanistan via Karachi. Interpol had been contacted, wiretaps had been placed but rather than move in and arrest him, it was felt that he would eventually yield bigger and better information if they sat and watched him and waited for him to make a mistake. Most of these guys knew they were being watched and were careful not to say anything too revealing in a phone conversation or in an email, but occasionally they did slip up.

As Clark read the files his face creased into a frown.

"What else do you have Neil?" asked Clark. The concern was obvious in his voice.

"I literally have hundreds of pages like that, all starting around Thursday evening right up until 2 hours ago. I think that whatever this is, its big enough that in order to organize properly, they have to risk open lines of communication. For smaller and for local attacks they rely on couriers, messengers and face to face meetings to coordinate. The fact that we're seeing international communications with some of the contacts here in the US makes me think they are planning a large multi-cell international operation with some if not all of the targets here in the states."

"Keep going Neil" said Clark as he continued to sift through the files.

"The last few hours concern me the most. We've seen a steep drop off in the amount of chatter, back to the usual levels and the topics are back to this sort of garbage that we see every day."

Neil handed him the translations that Bob had just given to him a half hour earlier.

"Jesus Christ Neil. This is happening in real time right now!"

Clark got up and began pacing back and forth in front of his desk. Suddenly he turned and reached for his phone.

"This is Gerald Clark. Requesting a secure POTUS line. Reference number 0032GC71."

Neil realized he was calling the Secret Service communications center, the acronym POTUS in Secret Service lingo stood for President of the United States. In situations where key administration officials needed immediate and urgent contact with the President, the SSCC provided a direct line to the chief agent with the President. Once the necessary voice scans and correct screening codes had been entered an agent would then notify the President and hand him a secure dedicated satellite phone. Now that the position of National Director of Intelligence was a Cabinet level post, Gerald Clark was one of a few people in the country that could make a direct call to the President. Clark waited a few seconds and then lowered his voice and repeated a series of phrases and expressions that a computer would analyze for accuracy in voice and recall. He waited a few minutes and then began to speak.

"Sir, Gerald Clark here. I have just been handed a report from our Director of Terrorism Analysis. We have a very real and credible threat that's just become apparent within the last few hours. I'd like to present this to you and the other Principals as soon as possible and upgrade our threat level to Red immediately"

6:18 pm Lackland Air force Base San Antonio, TX

The President hung up the phone and sighed to himself. There goes an evening with the troops he thought. These guys had worked hard to get an invitation to a banquet with him and he knew that it would be a big morale boost to sit down and shoot the breeze with them for a few hours. On the other hand he knew better than to question Gerald Clark's advice. Clark was as sharp as a tack and if was calling on the verge of panicking, there was a problem. He leaned over to the Colonel who had been giving him a tour of the Air traffic control center and said.

"Colonel, I'm afraid we're going to have to cut short our tour. Something's apparently come up that I have to attend to. I'd really like to come back and visit when I have some more time though"

The Colonel looked confused for a second but quickly regained his composure and thanked the President for his time.

6:25 pm Schaumburg Illinois

What a fucking miserable night he thought. It was not only cold, which he hated, it was cold and snowing. Marwan glanced around and despite his annoyance what he saw comforted him. Behind him stretching into the distance were the approach lights for O'Hare. These were set on twenty-foot high towers and spaced at one hundred yard intervals to give pilots a visual bearing as they made their approaches. Out in front of him lay the lacrosse and soccer fields for Schaumberg

High School. They were completely deserted and this hour. On a normal evening with clear weather, planes would have been coming in over the lacrosse fields every ninety seconds or so and then lining up using the approach lights behind him to find runway six. The storm however had interrupted the usual traffic flow and the planes were now in a holding pattern. He could occasionally hear them overhead but the cloud cover was too thick to see anything as yet. No planes had landed in the past two hours but if their luck held, that was about to change.

He and Mofiz had been monitoring air traffic control from their apartment all evening. Their apartment was less than a minute away and they knew from prior dry runs the approximate time when his plane would be arriving into O'Hare's control area. The storm had developed with astonishing fury and for a while it seemed that they would have to change to their backup plan. Then the weather had started to clear and they had heard his voice asking air traffic control to repeat themselves. Typical westerner they had thought, unable to obey authority, always questioning. They had then scrambled out the door into their van, and driven to one of the several sheltered spots around the airport that Marwan had already picked out in the weeks prior. As usual the planning had been meticulous. Marwan never left anything to chance and he had spent hours going over maps and charts looking for suitable locations. They had driven around O'Hare almost daily, discreetly recording traffic patterns, video taping flights as they landed and eavesdropping on the conversations of the air traffic controllers. Nothing was ever left to chance with Marwan Barghouti and he had planned for every possible scenario. The door to the van opened up and Mofiz jogged over.

"So did you get through to them" said Marwan.

"Yes, they're coming in just like you predicted, to runway six" said Mofiz

"How far away are they"

"About two and half miles now"

Marwan glanced at his watch…." Okay, that gives us about 90 seconds to get set up".

6:27pm Schaumburg, IL

The big plane broke cloud cover at around 2000 feet and they saw the welcome lights of O'Hare International airport. Even though John had flown into Chicago hundreds of times, he was still always amazed at the sheer size and dimensions of the airport. It was an immense facility, a full seventy-five acres with eight of the longest runways in the world criss-crossing it and feeding the airplanes into five huge terminals. Runway six where he was going to land, was off to the southern edge of the airport and the approach was directly over the town of Schaumberg. He could see that some people still had their Christmas lights up even though it was now mid January. John peered out ahead into the darkness and saw the bright orange line of approach lights below him that he would follow to runway six. At one thousand feet he started to bring the nose up slightly and adjusted the rudder to counteract some slight wind shear, nothing to worry about though. The air traffic boys had been right on the money, he thought.

A sudden movement off to his right caught his eye. There was a bright flare and then a thin trail of sparks arced up towards them in a pattern that John recognized instantly. One of the favorite pastimes of the residents around Bagram Air force base in Iraq had been to take potshots at the military planes as they were landing. John remembered nights where they would have to bring their B-1's into base in a tight corkscrew dive to avoid taking small arms AK47 fire. Most of the time it was just drunk locals pissed off at getting stopped at a roadblock earlier that day but occasionally it would be a hardcore insurgent firing an RPG. At night the AK-47 fire would show up as small clusters of light but the RPG's always left a telltale line of sparks that seemed to float upwards. The RPG's used by the Iraqi insurgents had been a remarkably effective weapon. It was essentially a handheld mortar tube with a grenade encased in jacket of thin shrapnel metal. When it was fired, the pin was automatically pulled so that in 4.5 seconds you were guaranteed a nice big explosion. This was what had made it so fearsome. You didn't have to actually hit your airborne target to bring it down, you just had to put it in the general neighborhood and the blast effect and shrapnel would do the rest.

"Christ John! What the hell is that" yelled Hank.

John already knew, but he couldn't believe what his eyes were telling him. Instinctively he grabbed the stick and began a hard roll to the left and brought the nose up to climb. The 747 however reacted sluggishly. It was powered down for landing and the flaps were extended to create maximum drag and slow the plane down.

"Raise the flaps and give me full throttle Hank! Someone's shooting at us"

Hank looked over at his Captain with a look of confusion.

"What the hell do you mean someone's shooting at us!"

Farnum ignored him and reached for the instrument panel. He flipped the flaps upward to begin retracting them and with his right hand pulled back hard on the throttle. Slowly the big jet began to respond, the nose swung upward and the thrust from four engines pressed Farnum back into his seat. But it was already too late. The grenade impacted on the right wing bounced off and a split second later detonated with a thunderous roar shaking the plane violently. The explosion sheared off the right wing entirely and punched a gaping hole into the passenger compartment. The two left engines continued to work, but without their matching number on the right, the plane flipped over and spiraled to the ground. American Airlines395 went off the radar screen at 7:36 pm and blew up on impact three hundred feet from runway 6.

On the ground by the lacrosse fields, Marwan allowed himself a brief smile. His modifications to the weapon had worked perfectly. The explosive component of the grenade had been upgraded extensively and the weapon that had just brought down flight 395 had enough power to destroy an Abrams tank. Mofiz pulled the car slowly out of the parking lot and in a few minutes they were on I-90 heading west. In the passenger seat Marwan closed his eyes and began to focus on what lay ahead. This assignment had gone well, his planning had been sound and had been executed flawlessly. Mofiz was proving himself a reliable partner. With Allah's blessing their work would continue. It had begun again..

Back in the parking lot of Schaumburg High school Janet turned to look over her left shoulder and saw the approaching lights in the sky Then something unusual caught her eye. There was a loud explosion and a burst of sparks in the field across from her and thin tracer line of flame stabbed up into the sky. Joey had seen it too and was now following it with his camera. With growing horror, Janet realized what she was seeing.

"Oh my God. It looks like something's been fired at that plane!" Before she could say anything else a huge ball of fire erupted alongside the plane and a split second later a massive concussion shook the ground. She screamed. Above her the plane staggered and lurched violently. A wing fell off and plummeted to the ground and a split second later its other engines still racing, the plane followed, impacting with a massive explosion that rattled the ground a half mile away.

Chapter 4

Maldonado looked around at the studio. It had been designed to resemble a law office. Behind Greyson's enormous desk there was a large cherry wood bookcase lined with legal reference books. The rug was plush and a rich deep maroon color. In the background an American flag fluttered in the breeze of a hidden fan. It was definitely meant to suggest power and influence and many of the guests, despite their own high standing were initially a little intimidated. Maldonado however was not. The studio lights came on indicating they were about to go live and the makeup people applied some finishing touches and ducked out of the way. Both men at this time were unaware of what had just taken place in Chicago

"Good evening General Maldonado." Said Greyson. "You look well, thanks for coming tonight"

"My pleasure Jim it's always a fun to come and talk with you" replied Richard

Seated across from Richard Maldonado, Jim Greyson was felt as if they had started the interview off on unequal footing. Greyson had expected Maldonado request that he call him Richard instead of 'General' and he was a little peeved that he didn't. Still he didn't let it show and continued on.

"You've been a civilian now for the better part of a year, what's been the biggest change for you." Asked Greyson.

"Jim, believe it or not the best part of my day is coming downstairs in the morning and not having an armed military policeman at my front door. As much as it was an honor and a privilege to serve our country I love having my privacy back again"

Greyson smiled and laughed, even though he was a little irritated at Maldonado, he couldn't help but like the guy.

"So you wouldn't consider serving again if you were called to in a different capacity?"

"Heck yes Jim, last month I was called to serve on the board of my country club's Greens committee and I accepted! Service is in my blood" The two men laughed heartily and Richard continued.

"Seriously though Jim, I do know a lot of good men and women like John Farnum coming back from Iraq that are getting out of the military and want to continue on in public service. My time has passed though and I'm ready to do things like offer advice, encouragement but nothing more."

Greyson knew that John Farnum had been rumored as a potential candidate for the Senate in Virginia. Nothing had been announced as yet but Greyson smelled a scoop.

"Folks the General is referring to Lieutenant Colonel John Farnum. He's a highly decorated veteran who flew the highest number of sorties missions during the two wars with Iraq. Are you still in touch with Farnum and do you think he'll run against Senator McNeil?

Richard smiled and said. " I do try to keep in touch with John, he and I talk occasionally but you'll have to ask him for yourself whether or not he's going to run. I can't think of a better person though if he does."

"General Maldonado. What advice would you offer your replacement, General Beamer? Since he's assumed command we've had a rapid drawdown of the force levels."

"Well General Beamer is doing a fine job. He's a good man and he will do us proud. When it comes to a force draw down though, you know my feelings on that already Jim. I think it's a mistake. We're allowing the Iraqi forces to bite off more than they can chew."

"But General, since our troops have started coming back home we're seeing, fewer attacks, fewer American and Iraqi casualties, we're..."

"Jim, let me interrupt for a second" said Richard, "It's true that those numbers you quoted look good and I'm thankful for that, but what I'm worried about is the long term consequences. What I fear is that now the terrorists have less to worry about in their back yard since we've gone. My worry is that without us out there on patrol they now have a safe haven like they did in Sudan and Afghanistan. Why bother attacking a few local Iraqi infantrymen when they can settle down and train for and plan a major attack on us."

One of the big differences between the two men was their feelings on how best to pursue the next phase of the war in Iraq. Maldonado was a vocal supporter of staying the course, whereas Greyson had ardently supported a decrease in troop levels.

"General that's a good theory but I have to say the facts don't seem to support it at all" countered Greyson. "The President feels that by having a smaller exposure abroad we decrease our profile and make ourselves a less inviting target. By leaving the battlefield we've denied them a fight that they were spoiling for. It's difficult to recruit suicide bombers when there's no longer a cause for them to die for!"

Richard smiled and shook his head wearily. "Jim believe me I've had this debate several times at the highest levels and while that last part is true, my feeling is we need to keep them occupied at all times. We have the capabilities to sustain this campaign indefinitely. They don't. We can keep coming back day in and day out to hunt and chase them down, eventually they will get tired, lose interest and want to go back home. Right now they're running on fumes and we're giving them new life by taking the boot off their neck"

The two men continued sparring back and forth for another 15 minutes neither one willing to give ground. A small red light started flashing in the studio, indicating to Greyson that their allotted time was up. He quickly wrapped up the interview and warmly thanked Maldonado for coming. Having a war hero on his show was always good for ratings and he had enjoyed the conversation tonight. Maldonado had stood up to him and defended his position well and despite their difference of opinion Greyson respected that. He found that too many of his guests just waited for him to take a position and then went along with whatever he said. As Maldonado walked out of the studio, Greyson turned to his assistant and started to ask about their next guest. He had a three minute commercial break and then they would be back on live TV. Suddenly there was a commotion in the control booth and the producer ran over to him.

"Jim it looks like we're going to have to cancel your next segment. We're getting word from Chicago that a jet just went down at O'Hare. We'll need you to go live with that right away."

"Holy shit!" said Greyson, "Do we have any other details on this…you know the how and when"

"All we know so far is that it's a flight out of London, the weather was bad but I'm also hearing that there's footage of a missile hitting the plane!"

The color drained from Greyson's face.

"Is this confirmed" he asked "I mean you're asking me to go on the air and tell the American public that one of their planes has been shot down on home soil. What if we're wrong?'

"Listen screw that Jim. We've got 2 minutes before you're back on the air; none of the other major networks have picked up on this as yet. We've got a chance to be up and running before CNN can get their heads out of their asses"

6:45 pm Langley Virginia.

Neil sat in silence while Gerald Clark continued to peer over the files Neil had brought him. The CIA headquarters at

Langley was laid out similar to the Pentagon but on a much smaller scale. The inner core rings contained the most sensitive offices and the security cordon grew tighter as you approached the center. The Director's office was located in a suite of VIP offices on the top floor and was under 24 hour armed guard. The only noise Neil could hear now was the occasional scuffing of the sentries' boots as they patrolled the hallway. As usual there were two television sets on at all times in Clark's office. They were always tuned to the news channels but right now the volume was muted as they waited. Clark had called for a Coast Guard chopper, which was the only one available on short notice and they were to fly directly to Lackland in San Antonio to meet with the President who wanted a face to face meeting before making a decision. It was shaping up to be a very long week. Neil smiled ruefully to himself. It was nights like this that had doomed his marriage six years ago. The unpredictable hours, the late nights and especially the secrecy had finally proved too much for his wife to deal with. The divorce had been relatively quick and painless since they did not have any kids and Claire was now back in San Diego with her sister.

His pager went off, he looked at the number. It was Bob Gordon's extension back at his office. A second later Clark's pager started beeping as well. The men both looked at each other; it was never a good thing when their pagers both went off at the same time. Clark reached for his phone and punched in a phone number and said gruffly "Gerald Clark here. What is it?"

He listened for a few seconds his face showing increasing shock as the seconds ticked by.

"When the hell did this happen?" asked Clark. A pause and then "Okay we're on our way to see the President. We'll set up a video conference with you guys in 2 hours. Be ready".

Clark hung up the phone and said: "Neil you are not going to believe this but.. '

Neil who had been pacing back and forth had now come to dead stop in front of the televisions. "Yes I will Gerald! Turn around; you've got to see this!"

Neil rushed over to the remote control and turned up the volume. The two men stood in horror and watched.

On the screen Jim Greyson was speaking:

"The footage you have just seen is from our affiliate in Chicago WNSO. It was shot less than an hour ago. It would appear that a passenger plane, a Boeing 747 from what we were told, has been shot down in Chicago. The initial reports are that there are no survivors on the ground. Once again this has not yet been confirmed by law enforcement but you can see with your own eyes a missile being fired at the plane. We have with us, the reporter that was there and witnessed that horrific attack. Janet can you hear us"

Janet Kilpatrick still looking visibly shaken appeared the screen. She was standing in the middle of a large open field which was strewn with debris and still smoking wreckage. In the background firemen poured flame retardant on the fuselage and doused the surrounding area to keep the jet fuel from re-igniting.

"Jim, I can hear you."

"Janet can you tell us what you saw tonight?" asked Greyson

"Well Jim, we've had some bad weather in Chicago today and I was here to do a report on the flight delays at the airport. We had just gone live when a plane flew overhead towards the runway and then a missile came out of nowhere struck the plane and blew it up"

"Janet, have you been able to get any word on how many people were on board?"

Janet turned back to the cameras. She had spent the first few minutes after the plane went down giving live commentary to the broadcast audience in Chicago. They had been unable to get any closer to the wreckage but could clearly see bodies lying motionless in the snow. She was now emotionally worn out and wanted nothing more than to go home and pour herself a long drink.

"Jim, I'm not sure, but from what we've been told it was a typical full flight returning from London and fully loaded these planes can carry 450 passengers."

Greyson pressed on. "Janet, were you able to get any footage of the area the missile was fired from."

"We tracked the plane for the first twenty seconds or so and then after it crashed both my cameraman and I turned back to the area we saw the missile fired from but there wasn't anything there. We've already given copies of our footage to law enforcement to analyze and hopefully they will come up with some leads soon"

"Thank you Janet." Said Greyson.

"Neil, I want that tape at Lackland with us in 2 hours and we're going up to a code Red right now". snapped Clark.

"Okay the tape will be there, but what about waiting for the President" asked Neil.

"That's my next call but right now we're going on lock down."

Clark hunched over his computer and began typing out a series of text messages. The system had been set up so that the National Intelligence Director could quickly communicate with key law enforcement personnel throughout the country should a crisis arise. His text messages were encrypted by NSA computers and sent out via secure satellite communication links. He scrolled through a list of names on his screen and clicked on the ones who were to receive this message. From this point on each person notified would have ten minutes to respond with a personalized code acknowledging receipt of the message and they in turn would then get in touch with the people on their lists. Within three hours the entire country should have assumed a defensive posture and hopefully prevent further attacks. Al-Qaeda's signature was multiple simultaneous attacks on different fronts. They almost never did an isolated hit unless it was a targeted assassination so the risk was that they were about to be hit again and repeatedly.

7:00pm Union Station, DC

Maldonado was tired but pleased; the interview had gone well and he had been able to get John Farnum some free publicity. His debate with Greyson had not been too over the top and he had left on a positive note and was sure to be invited back again. It would generate a little buzz and momentum going into the spring campaign season. After a brief wait his train arrived at the platform and he boarded his commuter train back to the suburbs. The coach he was sitting in was initially almost full but as the train made its stops it gradually emptied out until there were only two other people with him. His stop was the last one on the line and was located just outside Mclean Virginia. Mclean was a wealthy enclave of manicured lawns and German sedans. Tennis courts and swimming pools dotted the backyards of the houses. This was the where the high powered lobbyists and lawyers that ran Washington retreated to in the evenings. Despite the fact that Richard was a four star General and had been one of the most powerful men in the military, it was solely through his wife's salary that they were able to live as comfortably as they did. Richard always joked that he had married up a few levels and when they had moved into their new neighborhood a few years ago, he had realized it was true.

Richard looked over at his two fellow passengers, sitting across from him. They were young probably in their early twenties were wearing jeans, UVA sweatshirts and large backpacks. Richard remembered them boarding the train in Washington at Union station, they had sat in total silence the entire trip. These guys looked like college students, not the type to be traveling into Mclean late at night. They should on their way to a library or back to their dorms. Richard's interest perked up a little, he had always been an astute observer of people and something about these guys got his attention. There were no connecting train or bus lines in Mclean so whatever business they had it was there in town....or here on the train. The train began to slow down as it approached Mclean and the strangest thing happened. Both young men closed their eyes and began to chant in low tones. Richard leaned forward straining to hear; maybe they were doing some kind of fraternity hazing ritual. As the train stopped and the clatter died away he begun to understand what they were saying.

"Allah-Akbhar, Allah-Akbhar, Allah-Akbhar, Allah-Akbhar" One of the young men turned to Richard and locked eyes with him.

Richard recoiled in horror and disbelief. As the commander of the war in Iraq, he had heard of numerous tales of suicide bombers approaching their targets, chanting in Arabic, "Allah Akbhar" or God is Great, but now he was the one hearing it, in person on a train in Mclean Virginia. His instincts took over and he sprinted for the door but the explosion was massive and ripped through the compartment and adjacent cars with horrible efficiency. Richard was blown headfirst through the train doors and onto the platform. His twisted and burned body would later be found at the base of the stairway leading up to the street.

Chapter 5

The fatigue finally caught up to Janet just before she reached her apartment. She drove back to her downtown apartment in a daze, still unable to believe what she had just seen. After the interview with Greyson, she was taken to a holding area at the airport. O'Hare like other large public spaces had their own small police sub-stations and cell blocks within the airport itself. For the most part they detained immigrants with forged documents, drunk airline passengers or pickpockets roaming the terminal but now it had been turned into an on scene command center. She repeated her story to what felt like dozens of law enforcement types each one assuring her that they would be the last one. Finally after the last statement had been taped she had been allowed to leave.

As she sat in her car in the parking garage of her building, away from the cameras and from the policemen, she allowed herself to cry. Joey her cameraman had offered to drive her home but she had refused saying she just needed to get some rest but the reality was she needed time to herself. Joey might have nice to be with on a night like tonight but he was too shallow, too immature and it would only make her job more complicated. When she finally stopped crying, she fixed her makeup, got out and headed to the elevators hoping they were empty. In her building privacy was valued but she still drew the occasional stare and whisper as people recognized her from television. Tonight however the only people on the elevator were a young couple and they were messily all over each other and didn't spare her a glance.

She got back to her apartment and headed straight for the bathroom. After all the blood and death she had seen tonight she felt unclean. Janet stripped down in a hurry, anxious to get into the shower. She was still wearing her sports bra from her earlier workout and peeled it off slowly. Her breasts settled heavily onto her chest tugging her forward. She glanced at the mirror and smiled. She maintained her body with intense lifting and cardio sessions at the gym and it showed. She had always been in shape but when she started training in the Israeli fighting system known as Krav Maga her body had changed dramatically. Her legs and torso rippled with muscles and there wasn't an ounce of fat in sight. She climbed into the shower and as the water beat down on her, the stress started to melt away. After twenty minutes of pampering herself she felt better and stepped out of the shower and donned her bathrobe. An old boyfriend had given it to her and she called it her peak-a-boo robe because it did little to cover her. Still it was soft and sexy and tonight she needed the distraction of those old memories. Janet padded over to the bar poured herself a straight Scotch and downed it quickly. That felt really good she thought, as the warmth spread through her stomach and abdomen. She glanced at her answering machine, the light was blinking furiously but she ignored it. It was time for a few more drinks and then she would lie on the couch, listen to some Tim McGraw and relax. Whatever interviews or questions people had could damn well wait.

Langley Virginia, DHS offices

Gerald Clark's office, which had been quiet just a few minutes with just Clark and Neil Burke present, was now swarming with activity. An audio visual team had arrived and had set up a video loop of the crash on the television sets. It now played over and over at ¾ speed. They were working furiously to enhance the first and last few seconds of the footage. The cameraman had picked up the missile when it was about 100 feet off the ground. The bright trailing plumes of sparks were still visible and would give clues about the type of propellant used and the size of the tubing. In the last moments of the footage, the camera had swung back downward toward a wooded area where they thought the missile had been fired from. So far they didn't have anything useful but hopefully with some digital manipulation they could get an image of a person or an automobile.

Neil had been in touch with the Chicago DHS office and they had already established onsite command at the airport, debriefed the reporter and cameraman and taken possession of the original tape. Airport workers were being interrogated and local patrolman were already going door to door in the surrounding neighborhoods taking statements. A region-wide all points bulletin had been put out and state troopers in Illinois, Indiana and Wisconsin were stopping anyone on the roads that looked remotely suspicious. Their best chance of making an arrest would be in the first few hours after the attack, that's when the adrenaline was still pumping and these guys would be jittery and liable to make errors. From the standpoint of whoever had carried out this attack, their best bet would be to disappear into the anonymity of a nearby big city and lay low. Neil hoped though that the instinct to run would be stronger and that they would take to the road and make a mistake. The shock of what he had just seen had swiftly worn off and now he was back in control. He was managing and coordinating the ground investigation and Gerald Clark his boss, was working the phones with the President and other high level administration officials.

So far there hadn't been any calls in to claim responsibility but it was still early. The most likely suspects able to train and co-ordinate an attack like this would be Al-Qaeda but as they had learned after the Oklahoma City attack, you had to take the domestic guys seriously as well. Thanks to the racketeer influenced and corrupt organizations act, better known as the RICO act, the domestic terror groups had been almost dismantled and were usually small time; a pipe bomb would be the extent of their capabilities. A sudden thought struck him;

Al-Qaeda loved to make propaganda videos of their attacks and use them as a recruiting tool. What were the chances that a camera crew would just happen to be there and film the plane being brought down? He made another call back to Chicago and arranged to have the reporter and cameraman placed under 24 hour surveillance.

" Neil you've got to go now, the helicopters to take you and the Director to Lackland is here".

It was Bob Gordon; he had come running over to the Directors office after frantically paging Neil and was now standing with Clark in the doorway. A coast guard pilot in an orange jumpsuit and goggles waited beside them. The men walked briskly out of the building, trailed closely by two MP's safeties now conspicuously off their automatic weapons.

Devon Street Chicago

Marwan glanced over at the clock on the table, it was now eleven pm and the second operation should have been carried out already. The young men chosen had been from Chechnya, selected for their ability to fit in and not draw attention to themselves. He had no doubt they would complete their mission. The Chechnyans had always been a ruthless bunch and felt they had a score to settle. Their cause had been ignored by the West allowing the Russian government to commit atrocity after atrocity. It had been easy to recruit and train these young men and they had been eager to die when they found out who their target was to be. He had been monitoring the news channels for a while but so far the news reports were dominated by the downing of the plane in Chicago. Nothing yet out of Virginia but that was sure to change shortly.

Earlier than night when they got back to the apartment in Chicago, he had been pleased to see his handiwork already all over networks. The quality was much better than they had hoped for and it clearly showed his RPG hitting flight 395. There would be no doubt in the minds of America that this was an intentional attack. The networks were bringing in the usual talking heads, retired generals and security experts to deliberate how this could happen again. It was the lead story on all the channels and apparently the President was due to make a statement shortly. Americans would go to sleep tonight knowing they were under attack and awake to find that the unseen enemy had not crept away but had struck them again while they slept. Mofiz had already retired to his room and was probably asleep already. Marwan knew however that he had one more thing to do tonight. He methodically set up the camcorder and lights and began to speak clearly into the camera.

CENTCOM Headquarters, Tampa Florida

"Where the heck is my Goddamn transport?" General Frank Beamer was in no mood for excuses. He rarely, if ever was in the mood for excuses, but tonight was definitely one of the times that a clear coherent answer was needed. As Beamer watched the footage from Chicago, he became absolutely enraged. His country that he was sworn to protect had been attacked again and it looked like hundreds were dead. What the hell were those guys at Homeland Security doing he thought? Once again we were just a sitting duck without any warning whatsoever. Beamer knew and respected Gerald Clark but right now he was ready to tear into him. VJ Patel the Secretary of Defense had contacted him and told him to be present at the meeting at Lackland AFB. More than likely they wanted him there to discuss the options for a military response. But to what, though Beamer, they needed to know who they were fighting and on what terms.

"Captain, did I stutter? I asked you where the hell is my goddamn transport plane. I've got a meeting with the President in an hour and I'd like to actually be there". Captain Tuttle, Beamers aide-de-camp, was responsible for his daily schedule and was accustomed to Beamers foul temper. "Sir they are done fuelling and we will be good to go in less than ten minutes"

"Okay lets go then. I want wheels up in five minutes" snapped Beamer and headed out the door toward the runway holding area.

Beamer strode down the hallway, in his mind going over what he would say. The planned military response for a renewed wave of terrorist attacks on the homeland was complex and multi-layered. It had been developed and refined extensively at the highest levels; it was a document that Beamer was very familiar with. In the aftermath of 9/11 the President had ordered the Joint Chiefs and their staff to consider the effects of a sustained terrorist campaign on the US homeland. The chiefs had concluded that for a prolonged and effective crusade to be viable in the US, the terrorists would need to have an extensive embedded network already in place. The network would have to be trained frequently and an effective communication and financing network constructed. The conclusion was that the only way for this to happen would be if another country threw their resources behind this group.

It was obviously too early to jump to conclusions but if this just an isolated one-off event then the military response was limited to the targeted killings of high level operatives that had previously been placed under surveillance. If however the US were hit by multiple coordinated attacks, the strategic thinking was that state level actors were involved. In this scenario troop levels in Iraq and Afghanistan would immediately be drawn down and mobilization for invasion of Iran, North Korea or Venezuela would commence.

Beamer grimaced and hoped that this would not be the

case. He had absolutely no doubts as to the ability of his forces to fight another major war if necessary. He also knew that all three of these countries had hardened their defenses significantly and learned their lessons from what had happened in Iraq. The North Korean defector Colonel Jong Il Soon had said that their doctrine of war fighting had changed tremendously and most countries now understood that their only chance in an armed conflict with the United States was to survive the initial attack and fight dirty. If they had any nuclear capability left over after the first wave of attacks, Seoul, Tokyo and Kobe were to be the primary targets for these warheads. After that they would bring the fight to American soil and start a campaign of terror attacks against soft targets. Beamer knew that a lot was riding of the next few hours and hoped he was up to the task. They climbed onboard the Lear jet and a few minutes later they were in the air streaking out over the Gulf of Mexico toward San Antonio.

10:00 pm Lackland Air Force Base, San Antonio

The secure room at Lackland was originally built in 1972. The Air Force had decided a year earlier to base a long-range bomber squadron at Lackland. This ensured that Lackland would automatically become a first strike target if the Russians ever decided to launch an attack. As such, a secure room, deep underground, was added to make certain that someone would be around to call the shots provided they made it inside before the bombs started falling.

The room itself was accessed from the basement of the main mess hall. A nondescript but well guarded elevator took them down thirty feet into the sub-basement. From there Neil and Gerald were led through a narrow but well lit corridor past four armed MP's. Heavy steel doors at the end of the corridor opened up to reveal a cavernous room with what appeared to be a small submarine like structure in the center. The "submarine" was the actual secure room and was made of ballistic grade high tensile steel. It was bolted to the floor with eight inch thick iron bolts and was built to be able to withstand a direct hit from a tank shell. The idea was the men inside would be able to maintain command and control of the long-range bombers even in the unlikely event that the base itself was overrun.

Gerald and Neil stopped for a moment outside of the secure situation room. They had arrived late and the President was already inside with the Secretary of Defense and General Beamer from CENTCOM.

"Okay Neil give me the breakdown of what we know so far. I'll give the President a synopsis and if he needs more detail, you're going to need to jump in" said Clark

Neil nodded, it would not be the first time he briefed the President directly but the stakes were obviously higher now.

"What we have is that the airplane brought down was an American 747 out of Heathrow. The flight manifesto has four hundred and fifty people on board and there were no survivors. The video tape at the scene shows an RPG bringing down the plane and the guys in ballistics are saying that based on the flare and trail they think it's a Russian made tube. Also they are getting faint images of a van at the edge of the airfield"

"What do we have from the ground team at Chicago?" asked Clark.

"We are working with the guys from over at the National transportation safety board. They're doing the nuts and bolts of the plane crash investigation. I've got Bob Gordon talking with the head of the NTSB every hour and he's keeping us up to speed." replied Neil.

"Good." Said Clark. "So far the President wants Homeland Security and the CIA to head up the investigation."

Neil looked up at Clark with eyebrows raised but Clark cut him off.

"Yes, I know its on US soil, and that's the FBI's territory. We're going to work with them but chances are this thing was planned and carried out by some foreign nationals and that's where we come in. I'm going to be talking with the FBI and the local police in Chicago and they will give you access to everything they have. What we need now is someone who can see the big picture. You've been the one tracking the communications from the bad guys so you've got a head-start when it comes to figuring out who did this. We'll be flying out to the Bureau office in Chicago tomorrow and getting everyone together then"

Neil stood for a second and digesting what Clark had just told him. In a nutshell the investigation was his. Clark moved along rapidly not pausing.

"Tomorrow's going to be crucial Neil,. Right now the trail is as hot as it's going to be and if we don't get something solid soon it could be years before we get whoever did this. You got anything else or are we ready to go in?"

"There's one more thing that Bob Gordon just told me. It looks like the flight's captain was John Farnum" said Neil

"Hold on a second, do you mean the same John Farnum everyone made such a big deal about when he retired from the Air Force?"

"That's him. Now I'm not sure if that's just a coincidence or not but we'll look into it."

"What do you have on the van?"

"Not much, the computer geeks are working on enhancing it but its too dark to get a view of the license plates"

"When will they have the plates?"

"Not for another week at least"

"Christ Neil, we don't have a week. You call them up and tell them to get off their butts and get us something to work with! Okay let's go and get this over with. We're going to get our asses handed to us anyway"

The men waited for a secret service agent to key in the access codes then entered the room. A oval shaped conference table dominated the space and was ringed by comfortable six tan colored executive chairs. Plasma flat screen televisions were placed on the walls on both ends of the room and were tuned into the now continuous broadcasts from Chicago. The President looked up when Neil and Gerald walked in.

"Gerald, Neil, thank you for coming. General Beamer was just catching us up on our military options if this thing continues and gets out of hand"

"Mr. President thank you for inviting us to brief you." Clark looked over at the President who appeared relaxed and glad to see them there. The other men in the room however were not so receptive. The Secretary of Defense, Vinoj Patel continued to stare straight ahead while Beamer glared daggers at them both. Vinoj Patel or VJ as he was called was known for his analytical mind and ability to reduce complex problems to simple solutions. He and the President had become friends while they were both Professors at Annapolis and had remained close ever since. When the President had been elected he had been able to lure Patel from his post at a Washington think tank to become the Secretary of Defense.

"So Clark what *intelligence* do you have for us this time" asked Patel. He still hadn't looked at them as yet and his voice was heavy with sarcasm.

"VJ, General Beamer let me bring you up to speed on what we found out this afternoon just before this attack." Clark said, ignoring the dig.

"About 48 hours before the attack we noticed a spike in the quantity of communications that we were intercepting. In addition to talking more, the messages were now hidden in some kind of code that we haven't seen before."

"So what did you guys do about it" asked Beamer.

"We have seen other upswings like this before and sometimes it's been important and other times it wasn't. Our analysts were a lot more worried about this one because the coding they were using was new and we hadn't seen it before"

"How was it different Gerald" asked the President.

Clark looked over Neil, who cleared his throat and said "Sir let me try to answer that one. When Al-Qaeda was planning other operations, they would switch over to a simple method that they had perfected. Essentially it was a numerical cipher used to encrypt a web address that was password protected. Their operatives would go to that site to receive specifics of the planning and the attack. It worked like a charm because it was simple and easy to use until the NSA cryptographers figured it out. We were able to stop the attack in Alaska before it got started because we cracked that code. I think they must have figured that out and changed to a new method. This new one appears to be a form of an old substitution cryptogram that uses passages of the Koran and the Bible. It's been incredibly difficult for us to deal with because the reference texts are so varied."

Clark continued. "So we struggled with this code for about a day or so and then just as suddenly as it started, the communications we were intercepting went back to the usual mundane stuff. Neil here, immediately put it together that these guys may have gone operational and cut communications, so he rushed into my office, that's when I called you but by then it was too late."

"Once again just a little too late guys. How about some real time intelligence that we can use for once?" asked VJ still seething.

"That's enough VJ" said the President.

" No Sir, I think VJ is correct to ask that question and I'd like to answer".

All eyes looked over to Neil sitting next to Clark.

"When 9/11 happened we were pretty much caught unawares. It was only afterward when we went through all of the data we realized that the usual communication patterns had changed before the event. This time we were able to pick up this pattern, recognize what was happening and notify the President. Director Clark went ahead on his own and started a Code Red upgrade. So we did spot the danger and we did take action to avert it."

Neil's eyes were flashing with anger, he had been working non-stop the past four days and his own frustrations were boiling over. Patel held his gaze for a few moments and then looked away.

"What leads do we you have so far?" asked the President

"Sir, we've been working on the video trying to enhance the last few seconds of footage. "After the plane crashes, the cameraman brings the camera back to the spot where they thought the RPG was fired from. It looks like we have a brief image of a dark van driving away. We have APB's out from Indianapolis to Milwaukee and we're stopping and searching every vehicle matching that description."

"What about the reporter and cameraman? They're the only eye witnesses so far, anything on them?" asked Patel.

"We debriefed them afterward and they didn't have a whole lot more to offer. They seem clean, but we've got surveillance on them just in case" answered Neil.

There was a soft knock on the door and Andrew Mahoney the Presidents chief of staff entered the room. From the look on his face it was obvious he had bad news.

"Mr. President this is completely unconfirmed as yet but I've just gotten two calls from staff members that live out in Mclean Virginia and they're telling me that there's been a huge explosion out there at the train station. There's fire trucks and ambulances everywhere and the local police chief is saying it looks like two trains and the entire station were destroyed."

Chapter 6

"Janet, this is Larry at the station we've gotten a ton of calls from the STAR News New York office, they want to do a live chat with you tomorrow on American Morning. I told them you'd be available, so make sure you're here by 10:30 for makeup and wardrobe. You did a really good job tonight Janet and I'm proud of you. Give me a call if you need anything. Bye'

"Hey Janet, its Joey. That was some pretty wild shit tonight. Just making sure you're ok; give me a call if you want to talk."

"Ms Kilpatrick. I'm Bob Gordon with the counter terrorism office at the CIA. I know you've had a long night but I wanted to touch bases with you again to see if there's anything else you might have remembered. The fresher the memory the more likely you can remember some detail that will help us out. We're going to be sending an agent out to talk with you tomorrow morning."

Janet deleted the messages, stood up and poured herself another drink; it looked like the next few days were going to be one interrogation after another. The press wanted to talk to her, the CIA and Homeland Security wanted to talk to her and as usual Joey wanted to get into her panties. The good thing was that she could probably get herself a network job out of this. If this interview went well in the morning, she would have two live national broadcasts under her belt. As bad as it had been to watch the plane go down, she had been lucky to be in the right place at the right time. As a reporter you made your living telling the world about other people's problems. No one wanted to hear feel good stories; the evening news was just a recap of all the bad things that had happened that day in the world. People tuned it to see the traffic accidents, the house fires, the IED explosions not the heartwarming stories of grandma turning a hundred or that the Girl Scout troop sold all their cookies. It was the blood and gore that brought them back night in and night out and now she was at the center of the biggest blood and gore story of the year. There was no way she was going to miss that American Morning interview tomorrow for some CIA crap.

She picked up the phone and made a call.

"Hey Larry, its Janet. How's it going?"

"Good. It's been one heck of a night here at the station and the phones are still going off the hook. I'm surprised you're still up, you got a big interview tomorrow morning"

"Yeah I couldn't sleep. Do you mind if I come over for a while. I need to talk about tonight, I can't get it off my mind."

"Sure no problem"

Larry sounded surprised. He had been flirting with Janet for a while but Janet had always remained cold.

"You know how to get to my place?"

"Yeah I came over for the barbeque last summer remember."

"Okay great Janet. Give me an hour to wrap things up here and I'll see you at my place"

Janet smiled to herself, this way she would kill two birds with one stone. She wouldn't be there when the CIA guy came over to bug her in the morning and maybe Larry might live up to his reputation among the secretaries as the "Italian Stallion" after all. Despite being in his late forties Larry Rivers clearly kept himself in impeccable shape and he had developed quite a following among the ladies and a few of the guys at the station.

She quickly packed an overnight bag and headed down to the garage. As she pulled away a dark sedan did a slow u-turn and followed her into night.

For Larry Rivers the night could not be going any better. They had gotten exclusive footage of the plane crash, Janet had just called and was going to come by for a late night visit, and it looked like there was something big going down in Virginia too. He was supposed to have been long gone but had stayed on to manage things after the proverbial shit had hit the fan. It was now almost eleven and they had been going hard for more than six hours. Fatigue was starting to creep in but there was still work left to be done.

"Brad do we have any contacts down in Virginia?"

Brad was the station intern and was proving to be a real find.

"I just got off the phone with them Sir, we should be getting a download of their coverage in a few seconds."

"Thanks Brad, load it up and let me know when you have it ready so I can look at it"

Larry reminded himself to get a case of beer for the kid, he was a great worker. Larry had been the news director now for three years. He had started off just like Brad, an intern fresh out of Loyola and had worked his up to camera-man, then editing and now producing the news. Back when he had first started out, WSNO was a typical small station that got most of its material from the big networks. They would put together an undersized evening news show and then get back to the family programming from ABC. In the late 80's the station owner had seen the winds of change coming and decided to copy CNN's twenty-four hour news only format. They added the name News One and styled themselves as the CNN of the Midwest. At first the going was slow and advertisers pulled out, but eventually the format caught on and they added stations in Milwaukee, Indianapolis and St Louis. Now they were a full fledged force to be reckoned with and were able to negotiate deals with the big networks

"Here we go Sir, this is the unedited footage. They've just

gotten it from the field and they're shopping it around now. It's pretty graphic"

Larry walked over to Brad's Macintosh and hit the play button. The camera was slowly panning along the outside of the train station. It looked like it had been a small brick building and all that was left was a charred skeleton framework. The cameraman then walked around the side of the building, through some thick bushes and came around to the rear. From there you could see a short concrete stairway leading down to the tracks and you got your first glimpse of the train. The first responders had set up huge banks of generator driven floodlight and the ghastly scene was brilliantly lit up. Policemen and fire crews were still working and seemed too busy to notice the camera shooting. The train itself was a smoldering black tube, the front end had been blown off and the sides of that car were peeled off like a banana. He could see dozens of white body sheets stained red laid over corpses and body parts. As the dead had been found they had placed them in a row on the platform. Larry counted 28 sheets in all. It was unlucky he thought that this had happened at night. If it had happened earlier in the evening the train might have been crowded and the death toll would have been higher. Still the footage was great and with a little editing and voice over from the anchor, it would be well worth buying it.

The train was a surprise; after the plane had been shot down he fully expected more attacks, but he figured they would be the along the same lines; big showy events that would panic the public. He had agonized somewhat over participating but had quickly realized that it had to be done. The reality was that a request from someone like Marwan was not so much a request as it was an order. If he didn't comply he probably would have been dead within a week. Either way he had no qualms now, he had been richly rewarded and if he had not have done it they would have simply found someone else. Anyway all he had done was to make sure that someone had been there to take footage of the airport tonight. The storm was the perfect excuse and no one had said anything when he had sent a news team out to cover it. Now it looked like he would reap an unexpected benefit with Janet. He would need to hurry home and get ready for her.

"It looks great Brad, why don't you get them on the phone and I can work out a purchase agreement with them. I'm going to head home pretty soon and get some rest"

"Mr. Rivers do you think there's a connection between this explosion and the one here?"

"Brad, I haven't the foggiest idea. We'll just have to wait and see what happens next"

Chapter 7

It was almost midnight now and the mood in the room had darkened considerably. All the men present had known and respected Richard Maldonado. His loss was going to be tough to swallow. Neil was stunned, within a four hour span two of the most visible faces of the Iraq war had been killed in separate attacks. Reports had come in from the Mclean police department confirming that General Maldonado was one of the dead. In addition there were now suspicions that it may have been a suicide attack. The first responders and EMS personnel at the scene reported finding least two bodies that had been decapitated. This was typical of the injury pattern that seen with suicide blasts. The upward force generated was often sufficient to tear the ligaments of the neck, separating the skull from the spine. It seemed entirely possible now that they were seeing the first wave of a concerted terror attack on the US.

Gerald Clark turned to the President " Sir I think we all agree that we're seeing the start of some kind of campaign here. There are only four groups with enough funding and organizational skills to pull off something on this scale. To be complete we'd have to consider ETA and the Chechneyans, but the most obvious suspects are Al-Qaeda and Hezbollah."

The President sighed and took off his glasses. "Agreed Gerald but the question in my mind is how did we just lose General Maldanado and Colonel Farnum in one night? That's a heck of a coincidence gentlemen."

"It may not be a coincidence Sir".

Everyone turned to look at Neil.

"Go ahead, don't leave us hanging"

"What if the real targets were Farnum and Maldonado and shooting down the plane and blowing up the train were just meant to disguise it.?"

"Good Lord Neil. What would be the possible point of all of that" asked Patel. "You mean to tell me they would go to all the trouble of arranging what we saw tonight. When they could just as well hire a hit-man to do the job." Plus why would anyone target those two guys."

"What if they plan to keep going after our leadership and command positions. I think that..".

Before he could finish his statement Patel interrupted.

"First of all Farnum was by no means in a leadership position and Maldonado is retired. With all due respect Mr. President I think we've got bigger problems to deal with tonight than getting sidetracked with these conspiracy plots. Don't get me wrong. I knew both of those men well. I personally pinned on Lieutenant Colonel Farnum's Silver star but the big picture is more pressing.

Clark nodded his head in agreement. "I think and hope that its nothing more than an awful coincidence but we've got to start thinking about out military options and what we can do tonight to stop anything else from happening"

"Gerald I think we need to contact the FAA and ground all air traffic and do the same thing with all commuter rail and Amtrak." Said Patel.

"I agree with you Vijay. We don't have anything to lose by doing that and if we can get all the planes in safely that will be a great start." Replied the President.

"Here's a thought, what if those guys want us to bring all those planes in at once? If they have other teams out there with rocket launchers it would be a shooting gallery for them." said Beamer

The room was silent. Neil though about that possibility then spoke up.

"I don't think we have to worry about that. The planes have to land anyway whether we order them grounded or not so all we can do is hope that the National Guard is doing a good job securing the airports and their perimeters. Also why start something like that in the middle of the night when its pitch black. If they were going to do that it would have to be a daytime job."

"What else can we do *now*! I'm going to be going on Television tomorrow to talk about this and I'd like some more specifics to let the public know we've got this under control"

The President looked around the room and was met with blank stares. They all knew that for now it was not under control and they would just have to wait and see what happened next.

Saturday Morning, Schaumburg, Illinois

"Mofiz we need to get going, are you done?" Marwan was impatient to leave, they had a long drive ahead of them. Time was of the essence but Marwan knew the last thing they needed to do was to get caught doing something careless like speeding. Mofiz came walking out of the bathroom with two small duffel bags; he was sweating heavily.

"I wiped down everything from floor to ceiling."

"Good, go down to the car, I'll drive. We'll need to be alert today my friend they're setting traps for us all over the country but what they don't understand is that we are the ones doing the hunting this time."

Mofiz smiled and hustled off to the car. The van would remain here in the garage if they needed it in the future but he doubted they would be back again.

Marwan picked up a large manila envelope off the counter and placed it in his coat pocket. Using his sleeve he carefully closed the door behind him and gave it one final wipe. They got into the car and headed out in silence, he glanced over at Mofiz who was settling into the passenger seat. Mofiz had come to him with impeccable credentials; he was originally from Pakistan but had traveled the world fighting for al-Qaeda the past six years. He had started off like most of the younger guys, in Chechnya; killing Russians to hone his skills. After proving himself there he had returned to Pakistan just in time for 9/11. Marwan wasn't sure what Mofiz had done between then and now but the fact that he had been selected to help out on this mission meant he had impressed someone very high up in the organization. As they drove Marwan was alert for any signs of surveillance, they doubled back twice, made random stops and only when he was satisfied that they were not being tailed did he head out across town to the News One studios.

The News One building was a four story brick building on Belmont Avenue. They circled the building once, looking for anything out of place but everything was quiet. Marwan pulled out the manila envelope from his jacket and handed it to Mofiz.

"Give this to the receptionist and tell her it's the footage that Larry Rivers is expecting."

Mofiz jogged across the street and into the building, a few moments later he walked back out and got into the car.

"They said he's not there but they will give it to him when he gets back in this afternoon"

"Not to worry my friend, we are going to visit Mr. Rivers right now and pay our respects to him"

Mofiz glanced over and raised his eyebrows slightly, he knew better than to ask questions, but he suspected that Rivers would not be pleased to see Marwan.

"From what I recall Mr. Rivers lives in Rogers Park, let's drive over and say hello"

As usual Marwan took anti-surveillance precautions and then made his way over to the suburb of Rogers Park. They slowed down in front of a large three story house and looked around. It was a typical quiet Saturday morning in the suburbs and the neighborhood was just waking up. There was a couple walking their dog, a woman out for a run and the man across the street was shoveling his driveway. They continued driving and then pulled over and parked two blocks down the street.

"Mofiz, we are here to tie up a loose end so to speak. Mr. Rivers has served us well but unfortunately his time has come and gone. I will pay him a visit and make sure he has a speedy end"

Mofiz nodded and waited for the details.

Marwan stepped out of the car and walked down the street back towards Rivers house. Mofiz had already driven away but would return in precisely fifteen minutes. Marwan knew that would give him plenty of time to deal with Rivers and allow the casual observer to forget that a strange car had been briefly parked in the neighborhood. Marwan knew that Rivers lived alone and did not have kids. From surveillance earlier that month he also knew that Rivers generally got up late on the weekends and headed to the gym around 11 am. If he had guessed correctly, Rivers would still be asleep, he would knock and if there wasn't an answer he would slip in the front door and finish him off while he slept. The video he had recorded last night would create more questions than answers and give them a little extra time. Marwan had no doubts about the likelihood of success of his mission but he also had no doubts that his time was short. The Americans had proven themselves ruthless about hunting down and killing operatives and he knew he would have to sever all ties and sacrifice himself to ensure success and not endanger the entire group. The thought of this filled him not with fear or even pride but with a perverse almost sexual pleasure. Marwan was a rare breed that truly enjoyed killing and

he knew that when he died he would be sure to take many others with him.

Janet rolled over and looked at Larry, he was still sound asleep. It was 8:30 am; she had to get showered and dressed for her American Morning spot. Larry had been a bit of a disappointment, he had lived up to his reputation size wise but he could use a little self restraint. It seemed like it was over before it got started; still he had potential and if she could calm him down a bit, the possibilities were endless. She glanced over at him and her eyes lingered on his abs and the bulge lying across his thigh. She was sorely tempted to wake him up but she knew she had to get going soon. She went out to the kitchen to brew some coffee and turned on the television. Larry had just redone the kitchen and it was tastefully appointed with the latest stainless steel appliances, granite counter tops and a huge island in the middle of the kitchen. A plasma screen TV was hidden within the cabinetry and smoothly popped up at the touch of a button. To her relief the endless loop of her watching the plane go down had been replaced. It looked like some train crash in Virginia was grabbing the headlines now. Even though she was glad for the publicity, it was becoming a little much to see her face plastered on every TV screen. She was just settling down to her coffee when there was a light knock at the door. Janet tightened the rope around her oversized bathrobe that she had borrowed from Larry and padded over to the front door. She went to the window and discreetly peeped through the blinds and saw a man in a Fed-Ex jacket standing at the doorstep. He had his hands in his pockets as if he were trying to stay warm. Janet briefly debated waking up Larry, decided against it and opened the door.

Marwan saw a brief movement of the curtains just as he had reached into his pockets for his skeleton keys. He caught a glimpse of a female face, and as the door opened he made a quick mental adjustment and with one smooth motion struck the door with his shoulder about where he figured the woman's head would be. He entered and quickly closed the door quietly so as not to attract attention. He had expected to find the woman flat out on the floor but to his surprise she was still on her feet and coming towards him. Marwan backed away slowly and quickly assessed the situation. The woman was young and attractive, probably a new girlfriend that Rivers had just picked up. She looked vaguely familiar but he couldn't place where he had seen her face before. He hadn't heard any other voices so Rivers was likely still asleep or in the bathroom. If he could end this encounter quickly there was still a chance for a tidy outcome. He glanced at the woman again and quickly feinted lunging at her, she reacted rapidly, kept her balance and kept circling towards him. It was apparent that this woman had some kind of training, her balance and footwork were exceptional and the fact that she was still standing after taking a blow like that to the head meant she had to be dealt with carefully. Marwan kept circling, but suddenly he slipped, his right foot catching the edge of the carpet. In an instant Janet had closed the distance between them, clasped her hands behind his head and began to raise her knee to deliver a knee strike to his face. For a split second her weight was balanced entirely one leg, this was what Marwan was waiting for. He braced himself and then exploded upward catching her between the jaw and trachea with his head, snapping her neck back and knocking her unconscious. Marwan consciously slowed his breathing down, he had been caught unawares by another person being at home but so far he had adapted well. Entry into the house had been smooth and he had rapidly removed this unexpected threat. The next few moments however were critical; he still had to accomplish his original goal and then figure out how best to deal with the woman. Suddenly a man's voice from the kitchen said "Janet can you tell me what's going on?"

Marwan heart raced as he quickly spun out of the doorway and silently crept over to the kitchen. "Well Bob, it looks like a scene from 9/11. There are bodies everywhere and there are still multiple fires burning from all the falling debris."

Marwan smiled to himself, it was just the TV report from last night. He glanced into the kitchen to make sure it was empty and stopped dead in his tracks. The woman he had just fought with was the News One reporter that had covered the plane crash last night. He ran back into the foyer to double check and sure enough it was her. Janet was a very striking woman and not easy to mistake with someone else. He looked down at her crumpled form. There was a trickle of blood from her mouth. It looked like she had bitten through her lip and loosened a few teeth but he hadn't hit her hard enough to do any real damage, just enough to incapacitate her. He walked back into the kitchen, unplugged the phone and then took the phone cord and walked back over to Janet. He quickly turned her onto her stomach and then bound her with the phone cord. She wasn't going anywhere soon.

Chapter 8

"Okay Jim, we've got a guy in a Fed-Ex jacket who just strolls up to the house, with no truck and no packages. Then he pushes his way inside and we're just supposed to sit here?"

The DHS surveillance team assigned to follow Janet Kilpatrick, were in the midst of a heated discussion. They were parked in an alleyway across the street from Larry Rivers house and had just observed Marwan walk up to the front door, knock and enter.

"Listen Craig, are you sure you saw him shove the door open?"

"I'm positive Jim. He lowered his shoulder gave it a quick shove and then went inside."

"You know it could just be a simple home invasion. We should just call the local cops and get them to handle it,. We can't afford to go in there and blow our cover!."

"Jesus Christ Jim! We have an eye witness, to what has been the biggest terrorist attack since 9/11 in that house. The same house that by the way just got broken into. I'm done talking about this…are you coming or not?"

Against his better judgment Jim got out the Buick and started to follow Craig across the street. He remembered he didn't have his Kevlar on, thought about going back for it but instead hurried to catch up.

Marwan had crept silently up the stairs and was now standing outside the master bedroom. The door was partially open and he could see the nude sleeping form of Rivers laying on the bed with the sheets pulled back. Marwan smiled, it would seem that Rivers had a weakness not only for money but also for blondes. Typical westerner, he mused, easily bribed and no moral compass to guide him. He paused for a second as he thought he heard a car door close but he couldn't be sure. He glanced at his watch and saw that twelve minutes had passed since he got out of the van. He would have to move quickly because he still had the girl to take care of downstairs. Marwan crossed the room to where Rivers slept and in one smooth motion he pulled out his Glock G19, attached the silencer and squeezed the trigger twice. The silencer was of his own design, and he had drilled extra vents on the sides to allow better release of the propellant gases and to slow down the bullet. If the bullet flew at sub-sonic speeds it would further reduce the decibel level by eliminating the small sonic boom of a supersonic bullet. With these modifications he had been able to lower the decibel level on the Glock to forty decibels, which was about the same as a door being slammed. The effectiveness of the bullet however, especially at close range, was unchanged as evidenced by the small pool of blood collecting on the pillow behind Rivers head. He turned and padded back down the stairs and stood over the still unconscious body of Janet. A slight smile flickered across his face as he prepared to eliminate her and then disappeared as he heard the unmistakable metallic clinking of he front door lock being picked.

Jim Standard was by nature a meticulous man. Cautious and not one to hurry, he went by the book. He was visibly irritated that they were definitely not going by the book and making a warrant-less entry into a private residence. His partner Craig finished picking the lock, eased the door open and gun drawn, made a quick sweep of the room and entered. Jim silently slipped in and indicated with hand signals that he would do a clockwise sweep of the lower floor. As he turned to close the door behind him a dark van drove by and briefly slowed down. The driver of the van locked eyes with him and smiled but kept driving. Recognition, comprehension and then finally panic set in as Jim realized it was the same van they had seen about 15 minutes earlier. It had caught his attention as the street had been quiet and few cars were out on the road. Frantically he wheeled around to warn his partner but it was already too late. The Fed-Ex delivery man had appeared silently and was standing between himself and Craig whose back was still turned unaware of his presence. Fed-Ex mans' gun was aimed at the back of Craig's head but his eyes were locked on Jim's and he had his left index finger over his lips as if to say "shhh" . Jim hesitated for a split second and in that moment Craig's head exploded in burst of red. An instant later and still with a look of panic and confusion of his face, Jim's chest was penetrated by a slow moving bullet and his heart pierced. He collapsed to the ground and a minute later was lifeless.

Marwan briefly considered turning back to finish off the reporter but decided against it. He had been forced to fire twice with the front door open and that would surely draw the attention of the neighbors. He knew that even if he were caught now things would still go ahead without him. The wheels were already in motion and now the tempo could only quicken. Still the longer he remained at large the more time and energy would be spent trying to track him down. So now as much as he hated to, he would have to pretend to run and hide. He ambled down the street, got into the van with Mofiz and they quietly and anonymously pulled away into the suburbs.

Chapter 9

Neil awoke with a start. He was thinking of the spring of youth. Operation Spring of Youth was the code name given by the legendary Mossad to a series of assassinations they carried out in 1973. A year earlier at the 1972 Munich Olympic games, eleven Israeli athletes were killed by terrorists from the Palestinian Liberation Organization. German police had launched a botched last minute rescue attempt at the airport and in a short time, managed to kill equal numbers of hostages and kidnappers. After a brief trial and a short imprisonment the five remaining terrorists were released by the Germans and transported to Syria and Lebanon. Infuriated by this, Israel's secret service, the Mossad, subsequently tracked down and methodically eliminated the remaining five terrorists as well as several other senior PLO figures. The operation was widely condemned but the message sent had been crystal clear. If you target Israelis, we the Israeli government will find you, punish you and anyone else who may have helped you.

Neil wondered if this could be the start of a similar type of operation run by terrorists but this time targeting Americans. Was it possible that there could be a group out there that was picking off high-level American military figures under the guise of a larger terror attack. It was possible thought Neil but the only problem with that was why bother going to all the trouble. Like VJ Patel had said yesterday it would have been much simpler to just plant a car bomb in the targets car or hire some dumb kid to do a drive by. Neil shook his head and pushed it to the back of his mind. Whatever was going on clearly was related to the intercepts and chatter his team had been watching for the past few days. He'd have to wait and see if Maldonado and Farnum were just unlucky and happened to be in the wrong place at the wrong time. He glanced over at the clock on his bed-stand and winced, it was already 9:15. He and Gerald Clark were due to fly to Chicago at 10 am to meet with the local homeland security office. He debated going for a quick run, decided against it and instead ran into the shower for a quick bath. Fifteen minutes later he was seated in Lackland's small departure lounge.

"Good morning Neil, I take it you haven't heard about what happened in Chicago this morning?" Neil looked up to see Gerald Clark striding over toward him.

" I haven't, but from the look on your face I'd say that whatever happened is not good"

"You remember that we put a tail on that reporter Janet Kilpatrick yesterday after she was debriefed"

" Yes, from what I was told she cooperated fully and really didn't have a lot to add" said Neil with a puzzled look.

"Well it looks like she went over to her boyfriends place last night. Turns out he's her station manager. Anyway our surveillance team followed her over there and reported that were doing a static observation. They reported arriving at the residence at twelve thirty am. They said that everything had been quiet all night long The last time they checked in was at about six am today.. Well their relief got to the site at eight am and found their car empty."

Neil frowned "This is not sounding good Gerald. What the hell happened?'

"To make a long story short, when they couldn't find them or raise them on the radio, they called in Chicago SWAT and did an entry into the boyfriends house. They found the reporter out cold on the floor. She'd taken a pretty good beating but was still alive. Both of our guys that did the overnight stakeout were killed. Neil they were done execution style one bullet, close range to the head. The boyfriend was the same way. Head shot from close range."

Neil closed his eyes and took a deep breath.

"Okay it looks like someone saw her on TV last night and realized there was a possible eye witness and came back to finish her off"

"My thoughts exactly" Said Clark

"But why didn't they kill her? They killed our two guys and her boyfriend but then only rough her up a little. That doesn't make any sense"

"I agree. Doesn't make any sense at all. So far we don't have any witnesses besides the reporter herself. None of the neighbors heard or saw anything unusual"

Neil frowned and said "Here's a thought. What if they were not after her. What if the real target was the boyfriend?

Clark rolled his eyes" Always the conspiracy theorist Neil.

"That's what I get paid to do. Think of conspiracies. Where's Ms Kilpatrick now?"

"Last I heard they took her to Cook County hospital for observation and that's where we're headed now. We're going up to Chicago anyway so you and I are going to personally do the initial interview with her"

Chapter 10

Another day, and another scorcher in Baghdad. The temperature was already 115 degrees outside and it was only ten am. Frank Buchanan was also somewhat hot under the collar even though his climate-controlled office was kept at a bone chilling sixty-five degrees. Buchanan was the third most senior Army officer in Iraq. He had recently pinned on his second star and he was seen as a young man in a hurry by the Army brass. Today however, was rapidly turning ugly. He had awoken to the news that his old boss Richard Maldonado was dead and that a plane had been shot down in Chicago. If that wasn't enough he had just been told that Sheik Sistani's office had called and demanded an urgent meeting in person. Sheik Sistani was a respected Sunni Sheik from Al-Tikirit. He came from a well established and powerful family and was one of the most influential men in Iraq. He held the relatively obscure post of Minister of Transportation but that was of his own choosing. He preferred to stay in the shadows and work the political backrooms. Buchanan sat at his desk and considered asking Sistani to wait until later in the day. Quite often the local politicians liked to show off their perceived power by demanding meetings with American commanders in order to impress a political foe. Sistani, while not very likable was not given to whims and flights of fancy. He had been the first large tribal leader to swear allegiance to Washington, which had been key in recruiting other factional leaders to the American cause. In addition his assistant had hinted that the Sheik was finally ready to talk about accepting control of Baghdad, a key precursor to the final drawdown of American troops in the country.

"Charlene, where's the meeting with Sistani?" asked Buchanan.

"Sir, its at his office in the ministry. His nephew just sent me another email asking me when you'll be arriving." Charlene was actually Major Charlene Anderson who served as Buchanan's personal assistant and coordinated his day and activities. She had recently been added to his office staff after he had been promoted to Brigadier General.

"Okay then lets get the helo up and ready. Tell them to expect us in an hour."

"Sir, I think we're going to have to go by ground today. That sandstorm yesterday has us grounded for the next 24 hours."

"Shit!" said Buchanan, "That means we wont be back here until one or two at the earliest".

Traffic in Baghdad was always a nightmare and traveling at street level always presented protection headaches for his security detail. The Transportation ministry compound was only 3 miles outside the Green Zone but the trip would still take a half hour.

"Tell Jim Davidson I want to be rolling out of the gates in 20 minutes"

"Yes Sir I will, but he's not going to be happy" replied Charlene.

"Ah....who's the one in charge here? Myself or Sergeant Davidson?" asked Buchanan with a smile. "I know he's a little bit intimidating but don't be scared... I'll talk to him if you'd like" Buchanan enjoyed teasing Charlene she was always a little too stiff and formal. That woman needs to relax a little he thought.

Twenty minutes later Buchanan was in the backseat of an up-armored Humvee. He had been outfitted for the trip with a flack helmet and a bullet-proof vest. His entire office was in turmoil because it wasn't every day that a two-star took to the streets of Baghdad. Normally high-level VIP's such as himself were shuttled around in either Blackhawk helicopters or on C130 transporters. Today, given the urgency of the call and who the call had come from, there wasn't much of a choice and a convoy of 9 vehicles had been hastily assembled. His Humvee was one of 3 that were designated for VIP use. It had a cocoon of 360 degree ¾ inch armor plating. The engine had been upgraded and now had a massive hemi capable of producing 380hp. The suspension had been stiffened and the tires were capable of running at 70mph even if they were shot out. It was essentially a miniature tank on wheels.

Staff Sergeant Davidson who was in charge of his protection detail had rounded up forty other soldiers from the Military Police squadron to assist. He was, as usual, visibly and highly irritated. Since the surge of troops a year ago the security situation in Baghdad had improved but in his mind that just meant going from fucking awful to merely shitty. Moving a two star at street level here was going to be a nightmare but it was going to happen and promptly at that.

"Okay boys and girls we're taking the Boss to a meeting at the transportation ministry. This is going to be a VIP transport. Two hundred yard curtain from the prime vehicle to anything that looks or smells funny. Weapons safeties are off and you are to engage anyone and anything after issuing a single and I repeat single warning shot." Davidson looked around and was pleased to see he had gotten their attention. "Any questions... Good, I thought not ...lets go. The Boss is in vehicle four and I've got shotgun"

Four miles away Nouri Al_Sistani stood pacing around his ornate desk. It was said in the old legends that before you killed a King you had to prepare yourself to inherit not only his wealth but all of his troubles. Nouri, the eldest nephew of Sheik Sistani was beginning to understand what he had just put in motion. The thoughts of wealth, power and unlimited luxury that he had been promised were beginning to fade and the weight of his upcoming responsibilities loomed large. He, as the eldest related male would ascend to head his tribe. He as the oldest would then be responsible for avenging all the ills, rewarding all the favors that befell on, or were given to him and his family. Political patronage, managing family quarrels, having the final say on marriages, divorces; all the glory and all the mind numbing banalities would now be his. Pushing those thoughts from his mind he stopped pacing and forced himself to take a deep breath. The operation was not yet done and was not without great personal risk and danger. He had to be calm and ready to play his role. Gathering the necessary items from his top desk drawer he walked down the hallway and entered the ante-room of his uncle's office.

Sheik Al-Sistani played a crucial role in the government. Because of his standing as the leader of the largest Sunni tribe in Tikrit province, he had tremendous influence. In the chaotic post-Saddam Iraq, most Iraqi's had returned to following old tribal and religious allegiances. Saddam had tried to but had never been able to fully stamp out the importance of the tribe in Iraq. The Sistani's came from a legendary Sunni clan with direct links to the fourth Imam. It was said that Mahmoud Al-Sistani was one of two others chosen by the 4th Imam to be present when he was martyred. Such high standing could never be bought. The blood that flowed in Nouri's veins was the same blood that flowed in a man who had been honored by a descendant of the prophet. His lineage ensured immediate respect and with his uncle safely out of the way, he could emerge from the shadows that he was forced to inhabit.

The convoy had now left the confines of the green zone and was making its way through the serpentine maze of streets and alleyways that was central Baghdad. General Buchanan sat quietly in the back of his Humvee. Next to him Major Anderson was going over some intelligence files to prepare for their meeting. The street they were on was a relatively large one for central Baghdad. It had two lanes with a bright yellow double line running down the middle and was lined on either side by small restaurants and Internet cafes. The sidewalk was already crowded with vendors hawking everything from mp3 players and ipods to knockoff Luis Vuitton hand-bags. Their convoy rode directly up the middle of the street, with the 2 lead Humvees acting as traffic cops and clearing the way. The local drivers who were by now accustomed to these disruptions, got out of the way quickly with no questions asked. Most of them even went so far as to extend their hands out of their car windows to show that they were not armed. A key concept of the protection principle was that some part of the convoy must always be moving When forward progress was stalled, some of the vehicles did tight turns and figure of eights within the convoy itself. It was designed to keep insurgents guessing and randomize their movements. At the moment the forward vehicles had stopped to clear traffic along a side street. General Buchanan's vehicle was the one currently doing "crazy eights" as they were called but he remained impassive as the driver flung the Humvee into tight circles After they got past this congested area it was a fairly straight path to the Ministry building and safety. He kept a tight grip on the Glock G19 in his right hand. When they were traveling at street level everyone, even the VIP's were armed and expected to be able to lay down fire and protect themselves.

The first sign that there might be trouble came when Sgt Davidson looked up and noticed a large flock of pigeons directly above the convoy. Twenty feet above the rooftops a group of thirty carrier pigeons were swooping down and diving almost to the roofs of the cars and then at the last second arcing up into a steep climb. Pigeon racing was a favorite sport among the aristocracy in Iraq but recently the insurgents had started using the birds to send messages to each other and also to point out the presence and location of targets or enemies. Within the neighborhood someone had spotted their convoy and was now using the pigeons as a marker.

"Sir we've been made. They've got a goddamn flock of carrier pigeons circling right above us and we're still at least 10 minutes away. We can make it back home in about half that time and re-con a different route to the ministry. Permission to return to base sir?"

Buchanan looked out of the window and his eyes hardened he debated pushing on but in the end decided against it.

"Give the order. We're headed back."

"Listen we've been spotted and marked. Everyone take a heads up look" Davidson spoke into his headset to team leaders in the other vehicles.

"I want vehicle one and two to open up on those freaking birds now. The rest of us are doing a U-turn and heading back home."

The doors to the lead two vehicles swung open and the men poured out onto the street with their M16's ready. The tight staccato bursts of automatic gunfire were deafening and broke the relative calm of the morning. The mp3 and ipod vendors ran for cover and the Louis Vuitton vendors abandoned their merchandise for the relative safety of nearby buildings.

Buchanan glanced back as they sped away and saw a bizarre rain of blood and feathers falling from the sky and shook his head in disbelief.

"How the hell did they get our location so quickly. We've only been outside for a few minutes"

"Sir we'll address that in the comfort and safety of the Green Zone but right now I need to get our asses back to base."

Four blocks away Ahmed Reza heard the unmistakable sound of automatic gunfire and smiled. He was running full tilt toward the convoy and wearing the all red flowing robes that marked him as a martyr. The call had come on his cell phone one hour ago and he had quickly dashed home, prayed and donned his garments. His breath was labored and ragged as he struggled under the weight of his vest but he did not slow his pace. He knew others like himself were converging on the scene and he was filled with pleasure at the thought of the other Muslim warriors running fearlessly toward their deaths. As he turned the corner he saw the line of Humvees coming at him at break neck speed. His handlers had told him to let the first vehicle in a convoy go by as it was just filled with ordinary men following orders. He fingered the trigger mechanism and then a movement caught his eye. Another red clad warrior was already there and had just jumped out from the sidewalk in front of the lead vehicle.

Buchanan felt the explosion before he heard it. As a young infantry-man in Khe San he had been in the city when Air Force bombers had dropped daisy cutters to push back the Tet offensive. Even though he was across the river and at least 2 miles away he had felt the ground move and his innards vibrate. The explosion from the first suicide bomber brought those memories back with startling clarity. The driver of Buchanan's Humvee reacted as he had been trained to in the event of an IED. He floored it. The big diesel hemi shot them forward, hurtling toward the charred remains of the lead vehicle. The two other Humvees that were in front of Buchanan's did the same thing. There would be no time now to stop and help any survivors. The only priority now was to get the VIP back to the base in one piece.

"Trevor listen I need you to get us the hell out of here" screamed Davidson to the driver " You are not to stop unless Jesus Christ himself comes down and tells you to!"

"Sir are you injured?"

"No. I'm fine just a little worried that we're going to be late" Replied Buchanan with a tight smile.

Davidson turned back around and the last thing he saw was a curious looking young man in red robes running through the smoke toward them.

The armor plating protecting Buchanan's Humvee would have saved him had the explosion come from underneath the vehicle. The V-shaped underbelly would have deflected the force up and outward away from the occupants and he would have suffered at worst a concussion. As witnesses would later recount Ahmed Reza was able to leap directly onto the windshield before detonating his vest. The resulting explosion tore a hole though the armor plated glass and filled the interior with the other deadly contents of his vest. Nuts, bolts, nails and pieces of metal flew through the cabin with lethal ferocity instantly killing Buchanan and his entire protection detail.

Back at the Ministry of transport the two thunderous explosions rattled the glass windows of Sheik Sistani's office. Nouri and his uncle were seated on a large roomy sofa in the Sheik's office. The explosions had startled both men because of their proximity and intensity.

"Those were a little too close for comfort. Nouri make sure you check and see that none of our people were injured."

"Yes uncle I will but remember the General will be here any minute now. I will go check everything myself once he gets here"

"That's fine. Now what is it that our General Buchanan so desperately wants to talk about that he has to rush over here in the middle of the day?"

"His assistant will not say but I have heard rumors that he has been reassigned and called back home. Maybe he wishes to talk about his replacement"

Outside the eerie wailing of the midmorning call to prayer began.

"Well the General will have to wait while we thank Allah. Come let us go to the prayer room Nouri." The two men picked up their prayer rugs and walked down the hall to a large conference room. The other male employees at the ministry had already begun to arrive and set up for the second of five daily prayers that they performed. The room was dark, gloomy and poorly ventilated. The smell of sweat and tobacco from the other supplicants permeated the air. Most of the men were kneeling and were already deep in prayer. Nouri and the Sheik moved to the front of the room to the spots reserved for the tribal leaders. Nouri gripped the vial of yellow liquid tightly in his right hand. He had run through what he had to do a hundred times in his mind yet he was still nervous.

"Here, let me help you uncle, I know how your hands bother you" Said Nouri. He took the elder Sistanis' rug and bent over to unroll it. As he did, he snapped the neck of the vial between his fingers and let its contents spill onto the prayer mat. The two men then knelt and begun their prayers.

Pancuronium Bromide is a powerful drug used to induce paralysis and halt breathing. It is injected into patients before surgery to relax them and allow the anesthetist to insert a breathing tube. It is however always combined with a barbiturate to induce sleep before the onset of paralysis. Without the barbiturate the patient would still be awake and experience the onset of full body paralysis while the anesthesiologist was putting in the breathing tube. For Sheik Sistani the process of paralysis was a little slower since he was only inhaling the vapors spilled on his mat. The first thing he noticed was a blurring of his vision as his ocular muscles, the smallest in his body, relaxed. As he tried to bring his arms up to push himself erect, he noticed with rising panic he was no longer able to breathe. His arms remained stretched out in front of him in the supplicant position as he silently screamed for help. Around him, oblivious to his distress, the other men continued to murmur their prayers. The burning in his chest from air hunger grew more intense every second but he was helpless. Finally his bladder and sphincter muscles released and death soon followed. Beside him, Nouri waited another minute, his heart racing. The stench of urine and stool next to him was becoming overwhelming.

Finally he pushed himself up and screamed.

"Get us a doctor immediately the Sheik has had a stroke!"

Chapter 11

The trauma ICU at Cook County Hospital was bright and ultra-modern. There were fifteen beds arranged around a central nurse nurses station. Each room was large well lit with floor to ceiling windows and had glass sliding doors to provide some privacy.

Janet looked over at the nurse who had just entered her room. She was a pleasant looking plumpish middle-aged woman with blond hair rolled into a bun. She waddled more so than walked and the effort of crossing the room seemed to have winded her.

"Here you go honey, I've got some pain medicine and a sedative that the doctor ordered. It'll help you get some rest"

Janet stiffened. "No thanks I'm fine really. I'd rather not take anything right now."

The nurse who was accustomed to patients harassing her for more narcotics looked surprised.

"Are you sure honey? They told me that you got worked over pretty good, cracked a couple of bones in your face too."

"Believe me I can feel all those cracks but I'm doing okay. Save it for me when I get a look at myself in the mirror" Janet forced herself to smile but the effort caused the throbbing above her left eye to become almost unbearable.

"Fine by me sugar, but you just let me know when you change your mind. My name's Deb I'll be here till eight tonight." Deb turned to go then paused and turned around.

"Listen did you really see that plane get shot down last night.?"

Janet nodded.

"That's why this place is crawling with police. They told me who you were but you know on TV you look a whole lot smaller."

"Thanks, I guess" Said Janet and managed another smile despite the pain.

"You know Deb, I always wanted to be famous but right now I'm having second thoughts"

Deb smiled and left the room. Sitting right outside of the door were two uniformed officers from the Chicago police department. Inside her room but doing their best to ignore her were 2 plainclothes agents from the Department of Homeland Security. Janet had tried her best to talk to them but they had bonded with their blackberries and were busy texting.

Janet had awoken five hours ago to find herself in the back of ambulance on its way downtown to the hospital. There was a hazy period of intense activity in the ER and then she was wheeled up to a private room accompanied by her own security detail. She could recall going over to Rivers house, sleeping with him, and waking up the next morning. She had a vague memory of going over to open a door and then everything went black from that point up to the ambulance, Janet had given up trying to get any information from the homeland security guys. There was a big gap in her memory and no one wanted to fill it in for her, All they would say was that some people were on their way to talk to her. She asked about Larry Rivers but all they said was that his condition was stable and someone would tell her more later..

Someone or some people had obviously beaten her unconscious and probably put a good hurting on Larry as well. Did it have anything to do with the plane? There were so many questions and she was starting to get irritated by the lack of answers. Also she had yet to see herself in the mirror and did not look forward to seeing the damage she could feel that her face had taken.

"I'm going to the little girls room if anyone cares" announced Janet to no one in particular. The two agents glanced up as she slowly pulled herself upright, grabbed the IV pole and walked into the bathroom in the corner of the room. Her gown hung open at the back and Janet smiled to herself as she heard the texting come to abrupt end as the agents took in the show until she closed the door behind her.

Janet braced herself on the sink and then took a long hard look at her reflection in the mirror. It wasn't pretty. Her nose was puffy and crooked and there was dried blood caked in her left nostril. Her left eye was almost swollen shut and the eyelid was a deep violet blue color. There was a golf ball sized hematoma above that eye and when she opened her mouth she confirmed that had also bitten her tongue and lacerated it. Janet grabbed the sides of the sink in anger causing the veins in her forearm to bulge. Whoever had done this must have caught her by surprise. After all of her training and the years spent going to Krav Maga, she could hardly believe that someone could pull this off. She pulled her hospital gown up and looked down at her knees, they were uninjured; she glanced at her hands and elbows and noted they were uninjured as well. Those were her striking surfaces and the fact that she hadn't injured them meant she probably hadn't been able to get off punches or kicks. Unbelievable she thought looking at her battered face. All that training and with her first real test she had been knocked out, rendered helpless and hadn't been able to get in a single punch or kick.

She turned in frustration and walked out of the bathroom over to the homeland security agents.

"Listen when are these people supposed to show up and fill me in on what the fuck happened. You can't keep stalling me forever"

"Ma'am I expect agent Burke and Clark will be here in a few minutes."

"That's what you said the last time I asked" replied Janet, taking a step closer.

The agent glanced up and Janet and then over at his partner. A slight frown played across his face and for the first time all morning he put his blackberry down.

"Listen lady, we're not the bad guys. We didn't do this to you. We're here to protect you and keep you safe."

"You know I feel safer already" replied Janet, her voice heavy with sarcasm. At this point she was so frustrated she just wanted to lash out but she knew the price for assaulting a Federal officer would be high.

Just then a voice spoke up from the doorway.

"You should feel safe Ms Kilpatrick. From here on out you're going to have 24 hour protection at your side"

Janet whirled around as Neil Burke entered the room closely followed by Gerald Clarke. The two DHS agents scrambled to stand up and put away their blackberries.

"Relax gentlemen, I think Ms Kilpatrick has some real concerns that need to be addressed in private. Wait outside please"

The agents quickly glanced over at Janet and then each other and then walked out of the room closing the door behind them.

"Who the hell are you two?" asked Janet

"Neil Burke. I'm the Director of the Terrorism office at homeland security and this is my boss Gerald Clarke" Neil stretched his hand out Janet. Neil looked over at Janet and did a quick assessment. She was about five foot seven from the looks of it very solidly built. As he took his hand to shake it he noted the bands of muscle in her forearms and as she squeezed his hand he felt the bones in his hands start to buckle and he quickly pulled his hand away.

"Quite a grip you've got there ma'am"

"Yes I know." replied Janet dryly. "But what I need to know is what the heck happened to me last night."

"Okay we'll get right to the point but you'd better sit down first." said Neil, ushering her over to a chair. He sat down next to her while Clark walked over to the window and leaned against the window frame.

"May I call you Janet?" asked Neil. Janet nodded and Neil

continued. "After you were debriefed yesterday, we put a surveillance team on you partly for your own safety and partly because we have to assume that everyone is a potential suspect"

"The team followed you to Mr. Rivers house last night and reported that you spent the night there. Please be honest with us Janet and keep in mind this is a matter of national security. How well did you know Mr Rivers?"

"Well he was my station manager but I really don't think our private relationship is any of your business actually" retorted Janet.

"Unfortunately Mr. Rivers is now deceased. He was shot dead as were our two agents that were following you. You are the only survivor in a house full of dead people so it is definitely our goddamn business!" replied Clark.

Janet looked up with unmistakable shock on her face. She had figured that Rivers might also have been hurt but certainly not killed. Poor Larry she thought, he had been a good guy in his own way. Not someone she would ever have fallen for but still he had been a hard worker and was good at what he did. She struggled to comprehend what she'd just been told.

"Okay listen, I went over to Larry's house last night and we were intimate. He had been trying to get into my pants for a while and I'd always blown him off. But last night after everything I'd been through I just wanted to be with someone, no strings attached. But I didn't kill anyone" she said defiantly looking over at Clark. As much as she didn't want to Janet felt the tears begin to well up in her eyes.

"Janet we're not here to press charges or haul you of to jail" said Neil resting his hand on her arm, "We just want to hear from you what happened and what you can remember"

Clark pushed himself up from the window and walked over to Neil. " Neil can I have a word with you outside please"

The two men walked outside into the hospital corridor and Neil looked over at Clark expectantly"

"Listen boss I'm sorry if I took the lead. Do you want me to hang back? I'll be happy to."

"No its not that Neil, I don't care whether I'm the bad guy or the good guy. We both know how to do the good-cop, bad cop routine."

"You think she's lying or covering up?"

Clark shook his head" No I think she's genuine. Someone followed her over to Rivers house to finish her off. I think our guys maybe walked in when it was going down and the perps took off before they could finish her off."

Neil nodded "It's a little strange that our guys didn't call in for help and they also didn't get off a single shot. Its almost like they were ambushed"

"Well Neil anything's possible. But we've got a potential eyewitness in there so lets get back to work. Here's a breath mint big guy. I need you to work your charming little ass off"

Chapter 12

<u>Interstate 65 Lafayette, Indiana</u>

Marwan awoke with a start. He had drifted off to sleep after they had gotten onto the highway and headed south out of Chicago. A light rain had started falling and the wipers on the car were working rhythmically to keep the windshield clear. He glanced over at Mofiz and noted with satisfaction that were doing a steady fifty-five mph in the middle lane. In a few hours they would turn onto I-64 and head toward the East coast. They should be in Washington DC by tomorrow afternoon. That was the beauty of this country thought Marwan, the freedom to go anywhere and do anything. He would be able to slip into the capital undetected cloaked by the anonymity of sheer numbers. He thought back to this morning's operation and wondered if the woman reporter would be able to identify him. It mattered little though. From what he could tell they had gotten out of the city undetected and that alone had bought him at least another twenty four hours.

"Mofiz, you have the phone?"

"It is in the glove compartment"

"Good."

Marwan opened the glove compartment and removed the phone. As requested, Mofiz had purchased a pre-paid AT&T mobile phone. He quickly dialed a number that he had committed no memory months ago and waited.

"Hello" said a male voice at the other end.

"Is this the Egyptian doctor" asked Marwan.

There was a brief pause and then the voice replied, "The doctor is on vacation but I take his orders"

Marwan continued, "Good please tell him that his patients will be delivered in two days"

"Thank you"

The Egyptian doctor was a poetic nod to Al-Qaeda's number two man Sheik Hussein, who had trained as a hand surgeon in Cairo before becoming the spiritual adviser to Osama Bin Laden. Marwan himself had come up with the codes and passwords years ago and he was pleased that his contact in DC would recall it so effortlessly. The last piece was now in play and the circle was closing. So far they had encountered nothing but success. Allah had smiled on their plans and blessed them with good fortune. Destiny seemed to be on their side.

News One Headquarters, Chicago

"Holy Shit! Has anyone else seen this Brad?"
" No Sir I just put it in and started looking at it. I thought it was just some routine footage that Mr. Rivers needed editing so I opened it to get a head start and then this dude pops up"
On the screen Marwan was speaking slowly.
"It is for those reasons that America must not go unpunished. As such we the Islamic council of Clerics have decided to censure America and its citizens. We have started with your transportation hubs and struck at your aircraft, we have struck at your railroads and will continue to punish America until Allah his decided sufficient penance has been paid."
"Okay Brad I need you to make me a copy of this right away. I'm going to call the police."

The Pentagon, Washington, DC

Come rain, shine or national security crisis VJ Patel had always found time for his daily run and today was no exception. With long smooth strides he easily kept a seven minute mile pace and had already begun to drop a few of the larger secret service men accompanying him. The crisp morning air filled his lungs and with each breath he was able to clear away some tension from last night. For security purposes his run today was confined to the forested area on the southern perimeter of the pentagons grounds. There were a few dozen miles of well-worn trails here that wove in and out of the woods. The rolling hills and mild winter weather would usually have attracted large numbers of runners, but today his group was the only one out running. The events in Chicago and Virginia had galvanized the Pentagon staff into action. He however did his best thinking while running and not at a desk, so they would keep going for another few miles.

The meeting with the homeland security guys had not gone well. He had lost his temper, which was never helpful, but it seemed that those guys were always a step behind. After 9-11 he had sworn never to allow his country to be that vulnerable again. He thought back his last conversation with Richard Maldonado. It had been at a White House dinner for the Iraqi ambassador. Maldonado had been excited about his retirement and was looking forward to spending more time with his wife and family. He had talked about writing a book, playing golf and sailing in Chesapeake Bay and now he was dead. Neil Burke, the homeland security analyst, had brought up the possibility that Maldonado had been targeted individually. The President had also seemed to think it was plausible but the thought just seemed preposterous. His thoughts were noisily interrupted by his Blackberry pager going off. He unclipped it from his waistband, slowed to a walking pace and glanced at the number.

"Shit! What the hell is happening now" he muttered to no one in particular. He was being paged on the special secure communications line used only for top priority messages. All of the major phone and communications networks were required to keep a small percentage of their bandwidth open at all times. This was to ensure that in the event of an emergency, top military and government officials would be able to communicate immediately before switching over later to more secure military satellite phone systems.

The page was from Frank Beamer the CENTCOM commander who by now was back in Tampa. He quickly dialed the number and waited to be put through.

"This is VJ Patel" he said tersely.

"Sir please hold for General Beamer"

There was a moment of silence and then Beamers voice came on the line. "VJ I've got some bad news, we just lost Frank Buchanan over in Iraq. I'm just getting preliminary reports but it looks like his convoy got ambushed on the way to a meeting and a suicide bomber got him"

VJ stood rooted to the spot. His breath coming in short quick bursts.

"Frank, I think we need to reconsider what Neil Burke said last night. This may actually be some kind of decapitation operation against the military. Two generals and a colonel killed in 48 hours is no coincidence."

"My thoughts exactly VJ" replied Beamer. "I think we also need to worry about the President and the rest of the cabinet as well, and that means you too by the way."

"Listen I agree we'll need to step up security. I'll talk to Gerald Clark and the President but we can't afford to go crazy here and run for the hills."

"No I'm not saying that but we've got to at least convince the President to cut back on his public appearances until we get this controlled. You can talk to him VJ, you guys go way back and he'll listen to you."

"Okay Frank I'll do what I can. For now though put the Green Zone on lock down status. No one leaves or comes in except by air until further notice."

"Already did that VJ"

VJ managed a smile then hung up and looked around him. The woods were quiet, his security detail had set up a perimeter around him and were busy scanning the trees. They did this routinely anyway and for the most part it he had always found it amusing but all of it sudden it felt very reassuring.

<u>Cook County Hospital</u>

The trauma ICU was located on the third floor of the hospital and the Neil could see a group of children playing across the street in a small park. The day had begun to warm up and the snow on the ground was beginning to melt. He and Janet had been talking for an hour now and her story had not changed one bit. Neil had backtracked several times and asked her variations of the same questions several times but her story was rock solid. He got the feeling that she really wanted to help them but her concussion was preventing her from remembering everything. Several times she got and paced around the room holding her head in her hands as if willing her memory to return. He couldn't' help but notice the smooth easy fluidity with which she walked.

"So the last thing you remember for sure is going over to the front door. Do you remember if anyone knocked or rang the doorbell?

"I think I remember someone knocking but I can't say for sure."

"You mentioned earlier that you take a self defense class Janet. Have you been doing that for a while."

"Yes Neil! That's one of the things that really bothers me. It's called Krav Maga and I've been doing it for almost five years, so I'm actually very proficient at it. I train at least four times a week. I'm not exactly an easy target for someone to take advantage of"

"Well whoever it was that you let into the house must either be really lucky or really good to get the jump on you."

Clark who had been sitting by the window talking quietly

on his phone suddenly got up and said sharply "Get dressed ma'am we've got something you need to look at"

"What are you talking about Gerald? We can't just take her out of the hospital she's got a concussion"

"Well she looks fine to me" snapped Clark. "and we just had a major breakthrough. We got a call from News One. They got a taped confession delivered to them just now. Some guy is on there claiming responsibility for both incidents"

Janet looked over at Neil and smiled sweetly.

"Listen Neil I feel fine, just a little sore, plus the docs all said the bones would have to heal by themselves. They just wanted to observe me to be sure I was ok."

"There you go. She feels fine. We need to go look at this tape for ourselves and maybe if Ms Kilpatrick here gets a look at this guy it can help jog her memory"

"Okay" said Neil looking first at Janet and then to Clark "you're the boss"

Chapter 13

<u>Sunday Afternoon. George Washington hospital,
Washington DC</u>

The doors to the trauma bay slid open and Dr Mark Nawas quickly walked out into the chilly afternoon air. He was wearing only blue scrubs and a white lab coat and the wind bit into his skin. It was a typical winter day in Washington DC and the temperature was in the mid thirties. The sky was an angry slate grey color and held the promise of rain and sleet. After a shift Dr Nawas would typically hang out for a while with his Residents going over the days cases or just to shoot the breeze. He was well liked by the nurses and junior doctors for his easy going manner and his willingness to teach. Today however, his mind was elsewhere. As he walked through the parking lot to his BMW a light rain began to fall and he quickened his pace. Once in the car he took a deep breath, sank into the comfortable leather seats and closed his eyes. The life he had built for himself here was soon coming to an end. He had allowed himself to grow soft and enjoy the creature comforts he once denounced. Years had passed since the last contact and since then he had finished fellowship and obtained a full time position as a trauma surgeon at George Washington hospital. As time passed he had come to think, and sometimes hope, that he would be forgotten or even discarded. That was not to be the case. The phone call this morning and the brief conversation had sealed his fate and reminded him of the promises he had once made.

Dr Nawas was second generation Lebanese. His parents fled Beirut in the early eighties at the start of the civil war when he and his sister were infants. As he sat and contemplated what he had been tasked to do, he thought about calling his sister. It had been years since they had talked. The last time would have been after he had gotten back from London in

2001. His family had been so excited and honored when he won a Rhodes scholarship to Cambridge University. So it had come as a shock when he came back home wearing a beard extolling the virtues of Salafism. Tatiana was now ophthalmology resident in Boston and probably had her own life and maybe even her own family to worry about. It would not do her any good to call at this point. She would have lots of questions to answer anyway and there was no point in putting her under a cloud of suspicion by reaching out to her now.

As he drove out of the doctor's parking lot he wondered how it would happen. His contact this morning had asked for the Egyptian doctor and said that his patients would be there in two days. He had thought about this day many times in the past. Who would call, what was his mission going to be, how would he accomplish it? His job as a trauma surgeon at George Washington Hospital afforded him with unique responsibilities. It was the trauma center of choice for the capitol area. Whenever the President or his cabinet were in DC, this was the hospital they would be brought to for any severe injuries or trauma. In 1981 Ronald Reagan had been rushed in through the same doors he had just left. Dr Hill the trauma surgeon who had been on duty that day was his mentor and often regaled him with stories about the frantic moments in the ER when they all realized that this was not a rehearsal but the real deal. One thing however was clear; he was expendable. He had sworn to do whatever was asked of him and to take his own life afterward. The many hours spent at the London mosque had convinced him this was the only path to redeem himself and his family. His father who had fled his homeland and abandoned his religion was a disgrace. His mother who wore makeup and drank heavily was an embarrassment. His sister had always been pious and respectful and he felt a pang of sadness thinking about her but he had a duty to perform. A duty which would bring honor to his name and redeem his family in the eyes of millions of Muslims around the world.

After it was over his name would join the pantheon of martyrs who had sacrificed themselves in the fight for Islam. As he drove, his mind began to clear and his initial fears were soon being replaced by calm and tranquility. Finally his life could regain significance and vitality. Soon he would do more than save the useless drunkards and human flotsam that were his usual patients in the trauma bay. In a few days he would be called on to play a role that was pre-destined and he would be ready. He loosened his grip on the leather steering wheel slightly and allowed himself to smile for the first time all day.

News One Editing Room, Chicago

The convoy of black Suburbans pulled up with lights flashing outside of the News One Building. Janet was about to open the door when she felt Clarks hand on her shoulder.

"Hold on Ms Kilpatrick, we've got to get the all clear first. I have to presume that there's still someone out there trying to kill you"

Janet rolled her eyes but didn't try to get out. Outside the SUV a small phalanx of homeland security and local Chicago police department officers surrounded the vehicle and created a protective cocoon from her door to the buildings entrance.

"Okay, I'll go first then you and Janet follow right behind me" said Neil.

The three of them quickly exited the Chevy and under a dozen watchful eyes entered the building. They were met in the foyer by a tall, striking redhead wearing a neatly tailored pants suit. Janet thought she looked familiar but couldn't place her face. The woman extended her hand to Clark and said "Hi Mr. Clark. My name is Susan Kampton

I'm the stations' legal counsel"

Janet then remembered that she had seen the woman occasionally sit in on production meetings. Whenever the station was going to do a politically or legally sensitive piece Kampton had been brought in to help guide them around potential legal landmines.

Kampton then turned to Janet and her eyes opened wide. "Oh my God Janet. Are you okay? We heard what happened to you and Larry and its just awful" The concern in her voice was genuine and Janet allowed herself to relax a little. She had been expecting a little backlash at work. People were bound to gossip and while she doubted that she would be under suspicion for killing Larry, the fact that she had slept with Larry Rivers would now be out in the open.

"I'm as good as could be expected." she replied. "A little sore but I'm just thankful to be alive."

"Well we're glad to have you back in one piece Janet. Let me know if there's anything I can do for you okay?"

"Our editing assistant Brad has the tape right now. He's in the cutting room." said Kampton turning back to Clark.

"Before we get to the tape though I'd like to get a little background on how you guys got it." said Clark

"Brad came in to work this morning and saw a package addressed to Larry Rivers. They were expecting some footage from an affiliate, so he decided to get to work editing it."

"Do you know how the package got here to the station?" asked Clark.

"The envelope doesn't have any postage on it, so I asked the receptionist if someone had dropped it off and she said that a young man walked in this morning and gave her the package. He told her it was the tape that Rivers was expecting, so she just assumed he was a courier."

"Do you have any security cameras that cover that area."

"No we don't. I already checked that out"

Neil looked over at Kampton and smiled. "I'm very impressed Ms Kampton. It looks like you've done a little investigating already"

"Just trying to help out" she replied with a grin. "I don't think we've met yet."

"I'm Neil Burke. I'm the director of the Terrorism office at Homeland security."

The two shook hands and Janet noted that Susan's grip lingered in Neil's hand a second or two longer than necessary.

"Nice to meet you Mr. Burke and please call me Susie. I'll walk with you over to the editing area. Brad has everything cued up and ready to go"

Neil who was no stranger to having women find him somewhat appealing, had noticed Kampton's' extra attention and more interestingly, Janet's reaction to it. He made a mental note that he would have to try to regain some professional distance with Janet. At the hospital he laid on the charm pretty thick to get her to open up and cooperate but he didn't want to lead her down the wrong path. More than likely anyway she was just emotionally drained and looking for support.

The editing room was a small cramped space filled to the brim with computers, consoles, stacks of DVD's and computer disks. Brad had the tape cued and paused at the beginning of the recording and Marwan's face stared out at them as they gathered around the screen. Neil inhaled sharply but said nothing. He glanced over at Clark who was studying the face on the screen but he did not show any signs of recognition. Brad hit the play button and Marwan began to speak. His voice was soft, almost tremulous and his English had a slight middle Eastern accent but his words were clear. Neil stood stonily his face not betraying anything but he had instantly recognized the face on the screen. There were a few more lines around the eyes and the beard had some more grey in it but it was without a doubt the face of Marwan Barghouti. As he was sorting this out in his mind he heard a soft sob from Janet.

'That's him" she cried. "That's the man I saw at Larry's house this morning."

"Janet hold on a second. Don't say anything more." Neil

looked over at Kampton and Brad who were sitting off to the side. "I'm going to have to ask you to leave the room now guys before we go any further. We're going to need some privacy."

The three of them sat in silence as the others filed out of the room. Kampton tried to make eye contact with Neil but he was looking intently at the screen as Marwan continued his monologue.

The door closed and Neil looked over at Janet and asked "Are you one hundred percent sure that you saw this man at Larry Rivers House today?"

"It's still a little fuzzy but I remember going downstairs and then I heard a knock at the door. I went to open it and then all of a sudden this guy comes charging in and nearly knocks me over. I don't remember anything after that but that's him for sure!"

"Wow. We've got a huge problem here then. That's Marwan Barghouti; he was the chief military guy for Hezbollah in the nineties. The Israeli's think he was the one behind the wave of suicide attacks in Lebanon in 2001. They also think he personally carried out the hit on their tourism minister when she was assassinated in Paris. If he's here operating in the states then we're really in trouble."

Clark looked over with a puzzled expression. "Two questions for you Neil. How do you know that's Marwan Barghouti and secondly isn't he locked up in Syria now. I thought he pissed off the wrong people and Damascus decided to put him away for good."

"Three years ago he blew up a car in Lebanon. It killed a couple of prominent Christian politicians but the problem is they were meeting with a Syrian general who was in the car when Barghouti vaporized it. After that little episode Syria put him under house arrest and then moved him to a military camp out in the desert. It's not really a jail but they say he's under twenty four hour guard there. Its possible he could have escaped or just bribed his guards to take a nap for a few hours."

"Fair enough but this guy's been an mystery for years. We don't have any pictures or photos that I know of. How do you know its him?"

"Well its still just a hunch but do you remember that video that we got about a few years ago from that raid in Karachi. It was footage from a wedding in Pakistan. We identified all of the big name guests of honor at the head table except for one. The man that was sitting to the left of Sheik Hussein, the Egyptian doctor. We couldn't figure out who he was. He was obviously a bigwig since he was at the main table and right next to the Sheik but he didn't match up with any of our files on known operatives. Well I've been sitting around watching that tape in my spare time for quite a while. I got this bug in my head that we had to figure out who he was so I spent hours just going over it again and again."

"I would never imagine you to be the obsessive compulsive type Neil" said Clark sarcastically but with a smile. "So what do you find out about this guy in your spare time?"

"Well, at one point during the ceremony the imam starts to thank Allah for men like the lion of Damascus. The camera then cuts back for an instant to the sheik and he's smiling from ear to ear and clapping this guy on the back. It was just maybe 2 seconds of footage but the nom du guerre for Barghouti translates in Arabic to the Lion of Damascus."

"And you're telling me that the guy sitting next to the sheik is this character here" said Clark gesturing toward the screen.

"It's either him or his twin brother"

"Nicely done Neil but why didn't you tell anyone?" asked Clark.

"Well it's still just a theory and I haven't been able to confirm it yet, but if I'm right then what we've seen so far is just the start. This guy is a bulldog. He's relentless and he doesn't make mistakes.'

Chapter 14

The rifle had always been his favorite. Growing up in a small farming community to the north of Damascus his father had taught him at early age to be facile with a hunting rifle. He and his brothers would take the family dogs and hunt jackrabbits for sport. Even at an early age he showed a proclivity for killing and could easily outshoot his siblings. Of late he had been forced to use less elegant solutions. Explosives, bombs, poisoning and the like were all effective but they lacked the simple elegance of the long-range sniper shot. How appropriate he thought that it would be with rifle that he would strike his heaviest blow yet. Marwan closed his yes and imagined the shot in his mind. A headshot was the most efficient way to ensure a kill, but it was also the most difficult. You had to be sure to go directly between the eyes or just above the ears. Anything else would maim but not kill. A chest shot was the next best and much easier. Even if you didn't get the heart, as long as you hit the left chest, you were likely to take out something essential. In some countries where the medical facilities were poor, a gut shot was as good as a headshot. By the time they got the victim to the hospital and found a surgeon, the contents of the bowels had already been spilled internally and peritonitis would have set in, all but guaranteeing an exquisitely slow and painful demise. Here in the US with its fancy medical facilities and helicopters that could get a victim to a surgeon in minutes, a head shot might be necessary to do the trick. He sighed and closed his eyes. He would make all those decisions in due time tomorrow. His long rifle lay in the trunk, sleek oiled and black, ready and waiting to strike like a cobra.

NEWS One Station, Chicago

Barghouti's taped video statement was brief and to the point. In it he claimed responsibility for the attacks in Chicago and Virginia and promised more to come. Within thirty minutes DHS technicians were on site and had copies of the tape and lifted stills of Barghouti's face for flyers. An hour later Barghouti's image was being uploaded to law enforcement offices and databases around the country, and within ninety minutes Barghouti's face was on the screens of police cruiser computers from Maine to California. The decision to go public with his image was quickly approved by Clark and all of the major networks would be running the footage on their evening editions. America would sit down to dinner with Barghouti's face looking at them. Neil felt confident it would only be a matter of time before they caught him. Barghouti was operating in his territory now and it was almost inevitable that someone somewhere would recognize his face and call the police. Still Neil was puzzled, why would Barghouti personally claim responsibility, exposing his face to be seen by the world after a life of living in the shadows. He was also concerned he had never heard of the group that Barghouti claimed to represent, the Islamic council of clerics. There were a few things that did not quite add up.

"Gerald have you ever heard of these guys before? The Islamic council of clerics. That name isn't ringing any bells for me."

"Never heard of them Neil, but you know these guys form and reform new sects all the time."

"I suppose that's true but I still don't understand why all of a sudden he's outing himself like this. It doesn't make sense. This is a guy that has shunned the spotlight for years it's not his modus operandi to take center stage and claim responsibility."

"Neil you can ask him that and any other questions you

have when we find him. But right now we have got to get Ms Kilpatrick here some protection." Said Clark gesturing at Janet who was sitting quietly staring at Marwans face on the monitor.

"Normally I would object but after seeing what this guy did to Larry and your agents I'll take all the security you guys want to give. This guy gives me the creeps."

"Okay we'll put you in temporary protective custody until this thing is over. I'll get on the phone with the guys from the Bureau and they'll set you up in a VIP safe house. It's going to be a rough week or two until we get this guy Janet."

Janet nodded silently and then mouthed the words "Thank you" to Neil.

Monday Morning 8am George Washington Hospital ER

"Dr Nawas to trauma bay four. Dr Nawas to trauma bay four please" The hospital operators voice on the overhead paging system startled Mark Nawas. Was this the start of it, he thought. He had just arrived for his shift and was in the physicians changing room putting on his scrubs. He had spent a restless night thinking of the day to come and was still almost completely in the dark about his mission. When he had been a young student in London, inflamed by the impassioned sermons of the local Iman's it had been easy to pledge an oath of loyalty to the cause. He still believed their goals were just; freedom for Palestine and getting the Americans out of the Holy lands would always be near and dear to his heart. He stared at himself in the full-length mirror. In his white doctors coat, he stood tall and broad shouldered and still cut an imposing figure. The slight paunch in the middle and the grey that was sneaking into his neatly trimmed goatee were a recent but not pleasing development. Allah he prayed would give him the strength and resolve to carry out his sworn duty.

"Dr Nawas to Trauma room four please. Dr Nawas trauma four please!"

He quickly buttoned up his coat, grabbed his pager and walked down the hallway to the trauma area. The trauma bay was a large well lit room with a central nursing station surrounded by six trauma rooms. When a patient was brought in to George Washington this was their first stop. If they were in critical condition his team would do all of the initial stabilization treatments here and then head upstairs to the operating room. If they were stable and not severely injured he would do a quick once over and then send the patient off to the general emergency room to be seen by one of the ER doctors. It was change of shift time and nurses were busy giving each other sign out. As usual the place was a cacophony of voices yelling and heart monitors beeping. He walked into Trauma bay four and saw a thin young man on the stretcher clutching his wrist. Dolly Parker the grizzled veteran charge nurse looked up when he entered the room and handed him a green chart.

"Nineteen year old male skateboarder with a fall onto an outstretched wrist doc. He's got some deformity but he's neuro-vascularily intact. Can we send him over to the ER Dr. Nawas?'

Nawas smiled and said "Sure thing Dolly but let me at least see him first"

As he went through his cursory exam he noted a z-shaped deformity to the young man's wrist. A likely Colle's fracture he thought, painful but not enough to buy him a stay in the trauma bay. It would be off the main ER for this guy.

"Okay sir it's pretty obvious you've broken your wrist but everything else looks okay. We'll send you to the ER and those guys will splint it for you and arrange for you to see an orthopedic surgeon." Nawas turned to leave the room.

"Thanks dude, but how about a couple vicodins for the

pain before you hit the eject button. This shit is painful" the skateboarder moaned.

" No problem. Dolly can you give this young man one vicodin 7.5 mg tablet please."

Dolly rolled her eyes but said "Sure thing Dr Nawas"

Nawas doubted very much this young teenager would be the reason he was being activated. He had seen the incidents in Chicago and Virginia on TV last night and had no doubts that his contact from yesterday was tied into these events. No, he would be used for something on a much larger scale.

As if on cue his cell phone rang.

"Mark Nawas here" he said

"I know" said the soft voice in reply. "You come highly recommended doctor. Very highly indeed."

"Thank you"

"Are you ready to play a more active role after all these years doctor?"

Nawas swallowed hard. He could just say no and hang up now. It was not inconceivable that he could pack up leave and disappear to Honduras. Start a clinic in some remote beach town and live out a quiet life there.

"I'm ready" he said.

The voice continued for another minute, giving instructions and filling in details, then line then went dead and Nawas stared dumbfounded at the phone struggling to grasp what he had just been told.

<u>Langley, Virginia</u>

Marwan had allowed himself a moment of emotion earlier and he was not entirely pleased. He was walking through the woods to the south of CIA headquarters wearing shades and a tan colored camouflage suit. In a carrying case, slung over his shoulders was a lightweight aluminum rifle case. Mofiz had just driven away toward Andrews Air force base and Marwan had not been able to prevent himself from tearing up. It filled him with pride that there were men out there like Mofiz who could calmly set off on their own destruction without any hesitation. It was unlikely that the explosion at Andrews would do much damage but it would ensure that the base would go on high alert. Nothing in and nothing out for at least twelve hours. This would ensure that his package would be delivered to the right location. There were so many things that had to go right for his plans to come to fruition but so far everything had gone smoothly.

He reached the stand of trees he had scouted earlier and quickly scrambled up the last one until he was about twenty feet off the ground. From here the land gradually rolled downhill for two hundred yards until it reached a small stream. The stream itself was about fifteen feet wide and at its deepest point only knee deep. The far shore of the stream marked the outer edge of the CIA's property but the perimeter fence was set back another few feet from the waters edge. Once across the stream the terrain gradually sloped upward again. If he strained his eyes he could see a thin white line meandering down a hillside. This was one of the many running trails that ran through the grounds of Langley but more importantly it was the one favored by VJ Patel and his security detail for his daily runs. From his vantage point he could see about 30 yards of the trail from the point where it crested a hill and then disappeared back into the trees. That would mean about seven seconds of exposure to his target. Seven seconds to gauge the wind, adjust for the pace of his mark and sight a target from nine hundred yards. It was not an easy shot by any means but it would be done.

Marwan eased the rifle case off of his shoulders and slowly unzipped it. Inside it his Dragunov sniper rifle or SVD sat sullenly. He had hand painted it a matte black color and had mounted a customized optical sight which was he had also blackened. It was just over 4 feet long and weighed only 9 lbs with ammunition. It was not the best or most expensive sniper rifle but it was a low maintenance weapon and highly reliable. He had owned this one for eleven years and used it to great effect on numerous missions. When his "escape" had been arranged from Syria his rifle had been the first thing that he picked up in Damascus.

He positioned himself with his back to the tree trunk and his legs spread on a large branch underneath him. With his right arm he brought the rifle up into a firing position and noted with satisfaction that his shoulder was now also braced perfectly. He lowered the rifle and inserted a single 7.62mm Russian made cartridge. He raised the SVD back up into a firing position and glanced at his watch. It was now 10:12am and considering how rigidly VJ Patel kept to his exercise regimen, he wouldn't have long to wait.

He began his breathing exercises, inhaling slowly with the diaphragm and exhaling with his ribs. As he peered through the scope he began to slow his breathing rate down until he was breathing precisely ten times per minute, His whole autonomic nervous system began to slow and his pulse was now creeping along at forty-five. Marwan was one of a few truly rare people who when faced with physical stress reacted paradoxically. There was no fight or flight response for him. No burst or surge of adrenaline kicked in to give him an extra push to get out of harms way. His body simply saw a problem that needed to be solved and reacted in the most efficient way possible. The first member of the security team came over the hill closely followed by the lithe brown figure of VJ Patel. Through the scope he could see that VJ was wearing an orange long sleeve t-shirt and dark-blue tights. His lips were pulled back in a slight grimace. They must be pushing the pace today thought Marwan, He relaxed his shoulders, noted the lack of wind and imperceptibly shifted the SVD in his hands to anticipate where VJ would be. He exhaled, then slowly and smoothly squeezed the trigger and sent the bullet on its way. Nine hundred and eleven yards away VJ Patel who had boxed at the Naval academy felt what he could only describe as a massive upper-cut to the solar plexus. A split second later he heard the sharp report of the rifle but by then he was falling forward clutching his right side. In his tree blind Marwan put the rifle away, carefully climbed down from the tree and then walked out from the tree stand. Once out into the open he crossed his legs, sat down and observed with some satisfaction the chaos going on a half mile away.

Chapter 15

Neil and Clark had set up a temporary headquarters in a spacious conference room in the Chicago DHS office. It was now 10:30am and they had both already been there for an hour. Neil's phone rang. He looked at the display. It was a call from his office back in Virginia.

"Neil Burke here" he said. Neil then listened intently for a few minutes then his face broke into a smile. "That's great news Bob. Thanks a bunch". He hung up and glanced at Clark who in turn was looking at him expectantly.

"Gerald, It looks like my hunch about this guy being Barghouti is right. I just got a call from Bob Gordon down at Langley and he's saying they've got some preliminary stuff back from the ballistics lab."

"Go ahead" said Clark

"Well they were able to process some of the residue and it looks like it was fired by a Yasin rocket or something similar." said Neil

"Do you mean the Yasin rocket that Hamas uses against Israel" scoffed Clark. "That thing is a piece of shit, you couldn't a hit a barn door from 10 feet away with that."

"That's true but those are the old ones. Hamas is like the ugly stepsister to Hezbollah. They get the hand me downs that Hezbollah doesn't want anymore. About a year ago we heard rumors that someone in Hezbollah had made some serious upgrades on the Yasin. We hadn't seen any in action yet but the rumor was that Barghouti was heavily involved in modifying it" said Neil.

Clark nodded. "It looks like his fingerprints are all over this Neil."

"Did you hear about Frank Buchanan" asked Neil.

Clark nodded grimly. "That's a damn shame. He was a fine soldier and really making some headway over there"

"Gerald I really think this goes along with what I was thinking back in San Antonio. This could be a decapitation mission. For them to bring Barghouti over here and unleash him means something big is going down. If Hezbollah is willing to risk losing him then they have got to have something huge to gain in return,"

"You don't think this is a simple bomb and burn campaign do you?" asked Clark.

"No I don't. Too many big names are getting killed too quickly for this to be a coincidence. I really think we ought to think about getting the President and VP into a security zone."

"Christ Neil, you know we cant do that until we have credible evidence that he's being targeted. The secret service would have us locked up if we tried to do that." he continued "But I do think we ought to at least clue them in to your theory so they can make whatever changes they think necessary."

"Okay and what about the reporter Kilpatrick." Asked Neil

"We'll need to keep a close eye on her to make sure nothing else happens to her but right now if you're right then Barghouti's probably got a bigger fish to fry somewhere"

Emergency Room, George Washington Hospital

The much anticipated call finally came at 10:25am.

"Dr Nawas they need you on the EMS line stat" said Dolly his charge nurse. " They're bringing in a VIP and need medical control"

Nawas got up and with rubbery legs walked over to the Med-Com phone

"This is Dr Nawas at GW what do you have for us?"

"This is chopper-unit 435 we're flying to your facility with a fifty-five year old Asian male with a single gun shot wound to the right upper quadrant. Our ETA is fifteen minutes. The patient is pale and diaphoretic with a Glasgow coma score of seven. Blood pressure is seventy palpable, heart rate 115 and he has sonorous respirations."

" Okay 435 please establish two large bore IV's and administer a 2 liter saline bolus. Put him on one hundred percent oxygen and call me back in 5 minutes with a status update" said Nawas crisply. He paused for a moment and then continued,

"I thought for a second you guys said unit 435. Aren't you closer to Andrews? This patient sounds critical, you guys should be going to the nearest Level 1 trauma center, not flying him here!"

"Roger that Dr Nawas, but Andrews just went on full diversion. Some nutcase blew up a van full of explosives at their front door. The base is on lockdown now. No one in or out so you are our closest level 1. Also be advised that this patient is a VIP and will be coming with a secret service security detail."

"Thank you 435 we'll be getting ready. Call us back with any changes"

Nawas stood for a moment digesting the information. Fifty-five year old Asian male VIP; That would have to be VJ Patel. His injuries sounded critical to say the least. A gunshot wound to the right upper quadrant, pale and hypotensive. He was already displaying signs of advanced shock and was still a good fifteen minutes away. More than likely the bullet had hit the liver, which was bad, but there was a chance it may have also hit the inferior vena cava, which would be catastrophic. His instructions had been to keep the patient alive but if the bullet had nicked the IVC it would take more that just a good surgeon to save his life.

"Dr Nawas what the hell is going on? I just got a call from

the hospital CEO he's on his way down here and we have a van load of secret service agents that just pulled up."

Nawas turned around, his heart was racing and sure enough there were five secret service agents clad in black suits walking through the ambulance bay door.

"I'm not a hundred percent sure Dolly, but it looks like the Secretary of Defense was just shot. EMS didn't tell me but that's what I'm guessing. Tell the OR to get ready stat. Have them set up for an exploratory laparotomy and a right-sided thoracotomy. I want eight units of O-Negative blood down here right away! Got it?"

"We're on it Doc" said Dolly. She ran down the hallway to the OR barking orders to the other nurses along the way.

Nawas walked over to the nearest agent and extended his hand. The agent was a short stocky African American with a barrel chest and closely cropped hair.

"Good morning I'm Dr Mark Nawas chairman of Trauma Surgery. What can we do to help?"

"Morning Doc, I'm agent Carter with the secret service. We've been told to secure the area in a hurry for one of the principals."

"Can you tell me what's going on?" asked Nawas.

Carter frowned and shook his head "We're still trying to figure out ourselves doc but from what I heard on the way over here a sniper took out the Secretary of Defense and then a suicide bomber killed a bunch of people over at Andrews air force base. The whole of DC is in a chaos right now. We've got teams all over the place trying to locate the Cabinet and get them into custody. I've never seen anything like this before."

Nawas let out a low whistle "Unbelievable" he muttered.

Just then the med-com phone rang again. Nawas strode over and picked it up.

"Dr Mark Nawas here"

"Dr Nawas this is Unit 435 again with an update. We're

running into some problems here." Nawas could hear the stress in the paramedic's voice. The man was close to panicking.

"We have two large bore IV's in place and a fluid bolus going as instructed but he's still hypotensive and he just had a tonic clonic seizure. His respirations are slowing and his oxygen levels are decreasing. Please advise."

"Okay guys how far away are you?"

"We're about 5 minutes out"

Nawas did some quick calculations in his head and made a decision. The brain could survive without oxygen for three minutes and in this patient probably less than that because of his blood loss.

"I want you to go ahead and paralyze and intubate the patient and start a vasopressor agent to keep his blood pressure up."

There was a long pause and then the paramedic spoke up "Doc are you sure you don't want us to wait until we get there. This is a *really* big-time VIP here."

"I understand that 435, but if we wait too long to insert an airway and breathe for him, you'll be bringing us a body, not a VIP. I repeat, paralyze, intubate and start a vasopressor stat!"

"Ok doc your call. 435 out"

Neil closed his eyes and said a quick silent prayer that he had made the right decision. If he waited until Patel got here to start aggressive treatment it would almost certainly be too late, but if the paramedics were unable to insert a breathing tube after using the paralytic that would also doom Patel. Either way it would be touch and go at best.

Chapter 16

The news of VJ Patels shooting hit the Chicago DHS office with the fury of a hurricaine. Neil was pacing around the conference table in their temporary office.

"Okay now do you believe me Gerald!" roared Neil. "If it were up to me I'd declare martial law right now until we root out Barghouti"

"Well its not up to you or I, its up to the President, but if its any consolation the secret service have him in a secure location out in Maryland and the VP just took off in Air-Force 2." replied Clark.

The call had come in moments ago from the head of the Secret Service, Joe Sinclair. VJ Patel shot and in critical condition, Andrews air force base bombed and ten confirmed dead airmen at the scene. The news was grim and for Neil his worst case scenario was slowly playing itself out. Well at least they were taking this seriously now thought Neil. The secret service guys were implementing a code Grey meaning that all of the so called principals; the President, Cabinet, Vice President, leader of the senate and House Speaker were to be taken to secure locations immediately. A code Grey was the secret services' apocalypse situation meaning there had to be an active ongoing threat to the President or to multiple members of his cabinet. When this was activated the chain of command was to be located, separated and then secured, in that order. The last time this had happened was December 6th 1967 when Kennedy was assassinated.

"Well how come no one has come to get you? As head of homeland security aren't you part of the cabinet Gerald?' asked Neil.

"Technically I'm not in the chain of command so I get to fend for myself" said Clark with a wry smile.

The phone rang again, Neil reached over and picked it up. "Neil Burke here" he said.

"This is Joe Sinclair again. You guys are not going to believe this but we got Patel's shooter and it's the guy in the video that you sent us yesterday!"

Neil's eyes widened "You have Marwan Barghouti? Are you sure it's the same guy"

"Oh yeah its him all right. Patel's security team spotted someone sitting about a half mile away on a hill and when they went to investigate, he was there just sitting on the grass without a care in the world."

"Hold on a second Sinclair, Do you mean to tell me he was just sitting there, didn't try to get way or anything?" asked Neil.

"Yes its almost like he was waiting for someone to come get him. He told them his name and told them he had just shot the Secretary of Defense."

"Where is he?" asked Neil.

"We're going to hold him in the brig at Andrews for now."

"Great keep him isolated. No food, no water, no contacts. We'll be out there a.s.a.p."

Neil hung up the phone and resumed his pacing. Far from being relieved his sixth sense was screaming that something was desperatley wrong. We've been one step behind Barghouti all along thought Neil. What was this new game he was playing. First of all he knew Barghouti was an expert shot and even from a half mile away, Barghouti could easily execute a kill shot without any problem. Secondly if he did screw up and miss why did he turn himself in after botching it. Wouldn't it make more sense to go to ground for a while, regroup and try again another time?

"I'm flying down to Andrews Gerald right now! I know Barghouti's still has something up his sleeves."

Clark who had been digesting the news of Barghouti's capture nodded his assent.

"You go down there and bust his balls for me Neil. The President is in a secure location. The chain of command is intact and I personally think that now we have Barghouti we're in pretty good shape. We took a hell of a hit but I think its over"

"Listen to me I'm telling you there's more to come. I need to talk to Barghouti."

"Fine Neil, we'll get you down there today, so far you're the only one that's been able to keep up with Barghouti so have at it."

10:59am George Washington ER

The doors to the Ambulance bay burst open and Dr Nawas's heart sank. One paramedic was standing on the stretcher and doing CPR. He was drenched in sweat, his dark blue shirt stuck to his skin. The other paramedic held a blue oxygen mask and was busy bagging Patel through a breathing tube. The third paramedic along with a secret service agent clad in running shorts was laboring to push the heavy stretcher into the ER.

"Over here guys, bring him into room one" yelled Nawas. "What happened?'

"Well we intubated him and then right after that he lost his pulse and flat lined. We've been doing CPR for about two minutes now!"

"Okay lets get him off the gurney and onto a bed. Put him on our cardiac monitor and get me some size eight gloves." Nawas barked out his orders and the team of nurses and junior doctors sprang into action. One of the secret service agents stayed in the room with them and Nawas noted with some trepidation that the others had taken up positions outside of the room with their M-16's at the ready.

One of the nurses had produced a scissors and had already cut away Patel's running tights. She then grabbed the bottom of his shirt, which was remarkably unstained and cut it open. The bullet wound was a nickel sized ragged wound, located just below the ribs on the right hand side. Nawas donned his gloves and palpated the area. There was surprisingly little bleeding from the area, just a small red trickle. This would indicate that most of the bleeding was happening internally in one of the body cavities. The abdomen could easily hold at least four liters of blood and patients had been known to exsanguinate their entire blood volume in their pelvis cavity, which could hold several gallons of blood. Patel's abdomen however was soft. It was not distended and bloated, as it would be if it were full of blood. Suddenly another thought hit Nawas.

"Everyone shut the hell up for a second" he yelled. The room, which had been a hive of activity, fell silent as everyone looked over at him expectantly.

"Give me that" he said snatching a stethoscope from a nervous looking resident doctor. Nawas placed the bell of the stethoscope on Patel's chest and listened. On the left side he heard the reassuring whooshing of artificial breaths being forced in and out, So far so good he thought. He then placed the instrument on the right side and heard the unmistakable gurgling sound of blood bubbling around in the chest. That's it he thought, Patel's got a hemothorax, his right lung was full of blood and constricting the heart. The bullet, which had hit him in the abdomen, must have tracked upward into the lung and not downward.

"Give me some betadine, a chest tube tray and a scalpel. He's got a hemothorax.!"

"Its right here doc" said Dolly. "I set it up just in case"

Nawas looked up and thanked his lucky stars that Dolly was on today. A good charge nurse was like having another doctor working with you. She could anticipate things before they happened and not just react after the fact.

He donned his protective glasses and splashed the dark brown betadine cleaning solution over Patel's chest. He'd done literally hundreds of these procedures but his hands still shook slightly as he reached for the scalpel. Patel was in extremus now and if his life were to be saved, everything would have to go exactly right. There was no longer any room for second chances or second-guessing, every decision he made from here on out would have to be the right one.

Moving swiftly he located a spot two inches to the right of Patel's nipple and made a deep arcing incision down to the ribs. He stuck his gloved finger into the hole and swept it around feeling for anatomical landmarks. He was at the level of the 4th rib now and in good position. Next came the long blunt forceps and with a grunt he stabbed them through the rubbery lining of the ribs and into the chest. There was a loud audible whoosh and a gush of air escaped followed by a torrent of purple blood that splattered onto the floor. Nawas quickly stuck his finger back into the new hole to stem the flow and grabbed a large hose like chest tube. Removing his finger he inserted the tube into the hole and then fed about six inches of it into the chest. The results were immediate and satisfying. The cardiac monitor began a faint rhythmic beeping and the green flat line on the monitor began to show its first signs of heart activity.

"Nicely done doc" said Dolly. She bent over and hooked the chest tube up to a pleuro-vac machine that would suck the blood out and help reinflate the lung.

"We're not out of the woods yet folks. Lets get a quick chest x-ray and then we're going straight to the OR." Said Nawas. He took a deep breath and re-assessed the situation. He had bought some time by relieving the hemothorax with the chest tube but he would still have to operate on Patel. Gunshot wounds did their damage in two ways. There was the direct trauma caused by the bullet striking tissue, and then you also had to consider cavitation. Cavitation was the injury caused by the miniature sonic boom traveling thorough the body. Often this would cause more tissue damage than the direct trauma itself and it was especially lethal in high-powered rifle injuries. It was going to be a long haul for Patel he thought but he should be able to pull it off. But for what he mused? In the back of his mind he knew this was only the first step in the plan that had been laid out to him. If he could keep Patel going and get him out of the OR in stable condition he just might have the strength to be able to keep his end of the bargain.

Chapter 17

The F-16's circling at ten thousand feet were just above the cloud ceiling and not visible from the ground. If you listened closely however you could make out the low roar of their engines. They had just been scrambled with orders to shoot down, without question, anything that came within a seven-mile radius of the farm below them. On the ground, Army Ranger teams and secret service agents were spread out around the main building. All the roads into and out of the area were blockaded and armored personnel carriers were patrolling the perimeter.

The house and surrounding one hundred acres was owned by the President and had been in his family for generations. It had once been a working dairy farm but was now used as a weekend retreat for his family. The main farmhouse was a white wooden two story building set on a hill and overlooking a small pond in the front. To the rear of the house a large water tank overlooked the homestead. A horse barn was located a hundred yards away and was connected to the back porch by a well-worn foot-path. In the days before he had gone into politics, Andrew Wallace had thoroughly enjoyed coming here and pitching in to help run his farm. He was a big man and physical labor left him feeling invigorated. After entering the senate, he had not been able to devote anytime to his cattle and five years ago he had reluctantly sold them off to a rancher in New Mexico. He had found he was spending more time in the beltway than in the barn. After becoming President the farm had become an unofficial weekend retreat. Somewhere where he and his family could relax, out of spotlight and away from the prying eyes of the media. Now he and his chief of staff were in his wood paneled study in the midst of a heated discussion.

The President paced restlessly back and forth around his desk. It had been an unprecedented morning. He was on his way to address the Senate when word had come in that VJ Patel was shot. His motorcade had done a brisk u-turn and raced back to the White House grounds. Once there his chopper had materialized out of nowhere and within twenty minutes he was on his farm out in Virginia. The secret service had contingency plans in place for assassination attempts and when a Code Grey had been declared the nearest safe haven had been his family farm.

"With all due respect Sir, I don't think it's a good idea to go there just yet"

"Well what's the latest that you have from the hospital? I cannot sit here and hide while one of my closest friends is dying!"

"Sir the last I heard was that VJ just got out of surgery. Listen to me though. You cannot help the situation by going over to the hospital now."

"Didn't you tell me that they got we got this guy Barghouti in custody? If he's the out of the way and in jail, then I should be just fine."

"Yes I just got off the phone with Gerald Clark. They have Barghouti in custody over at Andrews and Neil Burke is on his way down from Chicago to interrogate him."

"Well that decides it doesn't it" growled the President. "If they have him in detention already then I'm safe. Lets get going we're headed to the Hospital"

Mahoney shook his head and followed the President down the hallway. It was impossible to argue with his boss once he got that look in his eyes. He glanced over at the secret service man next to him who was busy speaking into his earpiece and shrugged his shoulders. What else could he do? George Washington hospital was only an hour away by car so that would be, at most a fifteen-minute helicopter ride. Mahoney knew that fifteen minutes was not going to be enough time to adequately secure the route and the hospital, but he could only pray that the secret service guys were up to the task.

" Joe, I know you're not going to like this but I'm going to be going to George Washington hospital to see VJ". The President looked his senior secret service agent square in the eye to let him know this decision was not up for discussion. "I'll leave the details of how we do this up to you but I want to leave within fifteen minutes. After that we're coming back here and I'm going to go on the air, and let the American people know I'm safe and that their Government is still functioning"

"Ok Mr. President we're going to make it happen.". Mahoney and the secret service agent shared a brief pained look then they both grabbed their cell phones and started making the necessary calls.

Fifteen minutes later, an additional four Blackhawk helicopters had been fueled and launched from Andrews and were now in the sky racing toward DC. They would provide the aerial protection above the hospital while the F-16's would maintain close air support for the Presidential chopper as it made its way into the capital. Outside the hospital, the DC Police bomb squad was conducting a hurried search of the grounds. Sniper teams on the roof searched through their scopes for any hidden vantage points that could offer an assassin cover. Swat and sniper teams were coordinating with the secret service on how to cover all possible angles.

"Okay Sir we're ready to have wheels up whenever you're ready to go.". Joe Sinclair the head of the Presidents Secret Service detail had done his best given the circumstances. He could only hope now that this little side trip would go smoothly.

"Here's what we're going to do to get you in and out safely."

The President took a seat on the edge of his desk and folded his arms.

"Bill and Roger and I and going to be with you in the helicopter. Mr. Mahoney will be flying with us as well. We're going to land directly outside the trauma bay and from there it's a fifty-foot walk to the front door. Mahoney is going to go first and then the four of us are going to walk as fast as we can to the building." The President nodded for him to continue.

"The ICU is on the second floor, so we're going to take the back stairwell up one floor and then walk the East corridor down to the unit. We'll have agents in the stairwell and lining the hallways. If anything doesn't pass the sniff test we're going to muster in the basement and take surface streets back to the White House. Sir if we can spend no more than fifteen minutes with Secretary Patel we can probably get in and out before anyone realizes what's going on."

"Joe thanks for making this happen. I'll visit with VJ, pray with him and then get back here to the farm promptly."

<u>2:30 pm Andrews Air Force Base</u>

Neil was chomping at the bit to get to Barghouti. He closed his eyes and took a long deep breath and forced himself to stop pacing. Inside the holding room the MP's were securing Barghouti and setting up cameras to record the interview. It had been a while since he had done a hostile interrogation and he quickly mentally reviewed the process. He would first try to draw Barghouti into a narrative, allowing him to say and talk about whatever he wanted to. This would let him assess Barghouti's body language in a low pressure environment. In the next phase he would gradually ratchet up the level of intensity and see how Barghouti reacted to confrontation. If necessary he would resort to force, but only if necessary. Quite often the subjects need to boast and demonstrate their superiority made physical techniques unnecessary. His only goal today would be to find out if there were other immediate threats planned. Over the coming weeks and months, the CIA interrogators would have the luxury of time to break Barghouti. They would try to extract as much as they could from him about Hezbollah, its organization, its structure, its material and methods. That could wait. Right now, what he needed to know what was planned for later today or tomorrow.

"Okay Mr. Burke. He's all yours. Are you sure you don't want one of us in the room with you"

"Thank-you Master Sergeant, but I'll be okay. You guys can watch from behind the two-way mirrors. If he gets unruly feel free to come in and teach him some manners"

The MP smiled and took up a post at the door as Neil walked into the room.

Barghouti was seated quietly at a table in a metal folding chair. He was a small trim, compact man with a wiry build. He looked to be in his mid-forties but Neil knew he was actually fifty-seven years old. His hands were cuffed behind his back and his legs were manacled. A chain ran between the manacles and was looped into a thick metal bolt that was cemented into the floor. Barghouti looked up as Neil entered.

"Who are you?" he asked in his soft accented English.

The first thing Neil noticed about Barghouti was his eyes. They were a pale grey color and nearly blended into the whites of his corneas. The resulting lack of contrast almost made him appear to be blind. He had trimmed his beard and lost some weight but it was definitely the Lion of Damascus seated in front of him,

Neil walked around the table until he was directly behind Barghouti and patted him on the back.

"My name is Neil Burke, I'm with the Department of Homeland security Mr. Barghouti. Welcome to the United States. I must say you've been quite busy Marwan."

Barghouti sat impassively "I wanted to make the best use of my time here" he replied.

Neil walked around to the front of the table and sat on the edge.

"I must say I'm surprised to see someone of your stature here doing the dirty work."

"Mr. Burke, you have a saying over here in the West. If you want something done right, do it yourself. I was merely taking that advice to heart"

"You had to know that you'd eventually get caught if you came to the US"

Barghouti sighed and leaned back. "That's a risk I was willing to make. How can I ask others to sacrifice for our cause without being willing to sacrifice myself if needed."

"So what did you hope to accomplish this time by doing things yourself? So far this whole thing has been just a little news flash. Its over and you're sitting here in handcuffs"

Barghouti stiffened and straightened up but his voice remained soft and impassive.

"We have extracted payment in blood from those who brought death to our lands. Your terrorist commanders have been eliminated and your puppet politicians will soon follow them to hell"

"I doubt very much that anything else is going to happen. You know as well as I do that once the leader gets captured, everyone else just melts away. Its over isn't it"

Barghouti looked up at Neil with a look of bemusement.

"You can believe whatever you wish to believe. I might remind you that I was not captured."

Neil nodded in agreement. "That is true. It's not uncommon for criminals to give themselves up. Sometimes the pressure gets to them, they want to lighten their sentence, plead with the courts for mercy"

Barghouti shook his head and his voice hardened. "No Mr. Burke those decisions are still mine to make. You may control my freedom right now, but may I remind you that I chose to give up that freedom. And if I must die, it will be a decision I make with Allah, not with your courts".

Neil noted with satisfaction that Barghouti had become

irate. It was common for prisoners like Barghouti who faced life in prison to allude to suicide. It made them feel still somewhat in control of their fate.

"That was quite a shot you took. The secret service said that you were at least half a mile away. They are probably only seven people in the world I know of that could take that shot"

"Four"

"Excuse me? "asked Neil.

Barghouti had a smirk on his face. "You said seven people in the world could take that shot. That's incorrect. You forget that Patel was running. There are only four people in the world could make that shot and that includes me."

"Pardon me" said Neil with a smile. "I forgot he was running. So that would be Toth, and Miller from our sniper instructor school. Gonzalez in Brazil and yourself"

"Very good Mr. Burke. I see you are a connoisseur of marksmanship."

"In my line of work it pays to know who's exceptionally good at killing" Or almost killing thought Neil.

3:00pm George Washington Hospital

The rotor wash almost knocked him over as he stepped out of the chopper. Normally they would wait until the blades stopped spinning so that he could make a graceful exit, but today there was no time for those niceties. Above him on the roof of the hospital snipers scanned the ground and surrounding buildings for any activity. The President, closely flanked on three sides walked briskly from Air-Force one to the waiting open doors of the Trauma bay. As he stepped inside an agent to his left beckoned to him. "This way Sir" and held open a stairwell door. The President with Joe Sinclair at his side and two other agents in their wake, climbed one flight of stairs. At the top, a female agent was awaiting their arrival and opened another door for them.

In Patels room, Dr Nawas fumbled with a syringe. He only had a few moments now. The President would be there any minute now, and he was going to have to wait outside while President Wallace visited with the Secretary.

A secret service agent tapped him on the shoulder. "C'mon Doc time to go. The Presidents here. You can go wait in the conference room."

Nawas smoothed the sheets down and stepped away from the bed hurriedly.

The trauma ICU was at the end of this hallway and in it lay an unconscious VJ Patel. The President had known Patel since their days together at the Naval academy at Annapolis. The bonds forged then had led to a lifelong friendship that he valued. Their children had gone to the same schools and VJ had been a groomsman in his wedding. It was going to be exceptionally difficult to see his old friend like this he thought. To his left Joe Sinclair's pager was going off again, but Joe, locked in as always, was steadfastly ignoring it.

"Joe, you going to get that or not. That beeping is driving me crazy"

"Sorry Sir, I'll put it on vibrate." He unclipped the pager from his belt looked at it then put it away.

"Sir the ICU is right this way. Secretary Patel is in the first room on the left. We've cleared the area while you're here to just a skeleton staff to minimize security risks. The trauma surgeon that operated on Mr. Patel and two nurses are standing by."

The President nodded and slowly entered the room. Two agents were already in the room standing on the far side of the bed. The occasional beeping of the pulse oximeter and the rhythmic sighing of the ventilator broke the silence. Patel lay motionless on the bed with tubes coming out of every orifice. There were IV drips giving him blood, fluid and antibiotics. A bank of monitors above his head kept track of his and pulse, blood pressure and temperature. The President shook his head as tears welled up in his eyes.

He stepped forward, knelt at VJ's side and held his hand.

"VJ, its me Andrew. Can you hear me? I always told you that running was going to be the death of you."

He smiled wryly at his own weak attempt at humor.

"VJ I've known you for thirty years now and you've always been a fighter,. This is the biggest fight of your life now buddy so don't let me down. My old friend you can't leave us now. We need you more than ever VJ."

The President knelt for a few more seconds then stood up, still holding onto Patel's hand.

"You said the surgeon is here"

"Yes Sir would you like to speak with him?"

"Yes Please bring him in"

Andrews Air Force Base

"Lets recap what you've done so far and you tell me if I missed anything" said Neil.

"Shot down an airliner in Chicago"

Barghouti nodded with a smile.

"Blew up a train in Virginia"

Another nod from Barghouti.

"Bombed Andrews Air force Base"

Another nod and smile.

"Killed Sheik Sistani and set loose a suicide bomber on Frank Buchanan"

Barghouti grinned. "God is great. That was the one I was most concerned about "

Neil shook his head in disgust and continued.

"Shot and killed VJ Patel the Secretary of Defense."

Barghouti's face involuntarily tightened into a scowl, but he quickly composed himself and again another nod and smile. Neil had led Barghouti down a comfortable, rhythmic call and response dialogue. But Barghouti had stumbled when Neil had misdirected him about Patel. It was only a momentary facial twitch but it spoke volumes and the implications, if his interpretation was correct, were immense. Neil pretended not to notice but the reaction had been unmistakable. His suspicions had been confirmed. Barghouti's intention had not been to kill Patel but only to injure him. He had pulled off a shot for the ages and given the Secretary a non-lethal injury.

Neil's mind was racing now. Barghouti had implied that his capture did not mean the end of the operation. In fact he had come out and said that he had voluntarily surrendered. Patel should have been taken to Andrews AFB since it was closer to Langley but he hadn't been. They had taken him all the way to GW instead because Andrews had been hit by a suicide bomber and was on diversion. Barghouti was playing the oldest game in the book; the bait and switch. He had given himself up so that their guard would be lowered and the final act could take place elsewhere while they thought they had their man all wrapped up and safely in custody. This could only mean that trap had been already set at George Washington hospital and was only waiting to be sprung!

In front of him Barghouti had begun to cough. He inhaled rapidly through his nose and then coughed again. Neil looked up with alarm on his face.

"Are you okay" he asked

Marwan ignored him and kept inhaling and coughing rhythmically. Patel was dead. He had not survived. If Patel was dead then there was no way that Dr.Nawas could possibly succeed. There was no need for him to remain alive any longer. He had no intention of rotting away in a dungeon, held by infidels until he was a senile old man. Deep in his sinuses the cyanide capsule began to rattle around. He had done his best and would no doubt be feted as a legend for his deeds. Finally, the tablet, which he had lodged deep in his nose shook loose and fell backward into his mouth. He bit down hard and the smell of almonds filled the room.

Neil gestured frantically for the MP's to enter the room and grabbed Barghouti's throat to prevent him from swallowing but it was too late. The pill entered Barghouti's stomach and its deadly contents took hold almost immediately.

"Shit!" screamed Neil. The MP's burst into the room and one of them stuck his fingers down Barghouti's throat to try to make him gag, but Barghouti was already turning blue and frothing at the mouth. The MP's unshackled Barghouti and lay him flat on the floor. The characteristic smell of bitter almonds filled the air and Neil knew that Barghouti was beyond saving. The smell was overpowering now and Neil felt his own pulse begin to race. His own breath was coming in short ragged bursts and his face was pale and sweating.

"Forget him he's done" shouted Neil "He just bit into a cyanide pill. We need to get out of this room and out into the open."

The MP's dropped Barghouti's lifeless body onto the floor and the three of them raced down the hallway and burst through the rear door out in the open. Neil breathed in deeply, his lungs were burning but now he could wash them out with fresh air. With each breath he felt stronger and better. He looked over at the MP's, One of them was dry heaving but they were getting their color back and rapidly improving.

The sergeant looked who was bent over at the waist dry heaving looked up.

"Sir, what the hell just happened in there?"

"Barghouti somehow was able to sneak a cyanide pill. Didn't you guys search him?"

"Full body cavity search Sir. I swear he was clean from head to toe"

"Well I don't know how he did it but he managed to cheat us one last time. Goddamnit! Call your CO and tell him to send in a decontamination team to retrieve the body. You'll need to clear that wing of the building and set up a perimeter to keep people out until you can get the corpse out and ventilate that room."

The MP's staggered off around the building to find their CO and Neil then pulled out his cell phone and dialed Gerald Clark's cell phone.

"Gerald, Barghouti's got something planned at George Washington Hospital! We need to get Secretary Patel out of there and do a sweep of the building"

In the background Neil heard a fire alarm go off within the building.

"Neil what are you talking about? Did you get anything out of Barghouti"

Neil quickly briefed Clark about the interrogation, Barghouti's reaction to his ploy and subsequent suicide.

"I'll get on the phone right away with Joe Sinclair. He's taken personal command of the Presidents secret service detail. I'll make sure that he keeps the President away from the hospital and I want you to head out to GW, and get VJ out of there VJ as soon as possible."

"I'm on my way"

Neil snapped his phone shut and ran around to the front of the building. It was a low slung two story building painted in the same uninspiring tan and brown color that all Air Force structures are painted in. In the distance he could hear sirens approaching and as he rounded the corner he saw the main doors open and people started streaming out of them. One of the MP's that had been outside of the interrogation room was now hustling people out of the door and Neil jogged over to him.

"Good job Sergeant, as long as the body is in a closed room, the rest of us should be safe out here. Make sure to tell the decon team it's a cyanide poisoning so they can have the antidote ready in case anyone gets sick from the body."

In the background the sirens grew louder and more urgent. The flow of people out of the door had slowed to a trickle and only a few stragglers were coming out now. They all looked shaken and scared but none seemed to be suffering from any inhalation poisoning.

"Sir I really don't think that's going to be a problem anymore"

"What do you mean Sergeant?"

The sirens were now deafening and Neil turned to see two trucks come screeching around the corner with the letters RMPRT emblazoned on the back. Neil recognized the acronym stood for rapid military police response team, it the military police's version of a SWAT team.

"Well Sir, about the room. It's empty. We're not looking for a body anymore we're looking for a fugitive."

3:38pm George Washington Trauma ICU

"C'mon Doc, its show time. The President wants to speak to you"

Nawas looked up and nodded. He was sitting along with two of his nurses in a vacant ICU room. They had been debriefed by the secret service and suffered the indignity of a thorough body cavity search. The surgery on Patel had gone as well as could be expected. He had repaired a vena cava tear and removed fourteen inches of small intestine that was badly damaged but the bleeding had been staunched. Despite his severe wounds Patel clung doggedly to life and his vital signs had stabilized. It was a job well done and one that Nawas was justifiably proud of. Dolly his charge nurse got up to accompany them.

"No ma'am, you stay right here. Just the Doc" the agent said firmly.

Nawas stood up somewhat unsteadily. His knees were weak and his hands shook slightly. It was going to take all of his will to just walk into Patel's room. They walked down a deserted hallway, turned right and entered the main ICU ward. Patel's room was on the other side of the ward and Nawas could see two black clad agents outside of the door. They crossed the hallway and entered the room. He saw the President, his back to him, holding Patel's hand. Nawas had never seen the President in real life before and was surprised how big he was in real life. The two agents with him walked over to the President and took up flanking positions. Nawas broke into a sweat. This was it. His life his families' reputation, everything he worked for and had sworn to do was now on the line.

"Dr Nawas, I just wanted to say thank-you for working on VJ".

The President turned to Nawas and extended his hand. Nawas took it with both damp palms and grasped it and then stepped back.

"Sir it was on honor to do whatever we could to help"

"I know it's hard to tell, but based on your experience what are his chances?"

Nawas edged closer to the bed.

"Well its always difficult to make a prognosis but we were able to stop the bleeding and he is doing much better. Once we get past the initial injuries, infection is the other big worry"

Nawas then gestured towards the drips and took another step toward the bed.

"We have him on Rocephin and Imvantz which are two of the strongest antibiotics in our arsenal"

Nawas took another step forward and was now at the Patel's bedside and about three feet away from the President. The two agents, who had been behind the President matched his action and took a step forward as well.

Joe Sinclair who was behind Nawas, in the doorway scowled but took no action. Once again his pager buzzed to life vibrating furiously. This time it showed he had a text message marked urgent from Gerald Clark.

"It looks like your also giving him some blood" said the President.

"Yes Mr. President he's gotten eight units of blood so far to replenish what he lost. It's a good thing he was in great physical shape or he might not have made it to the OR"

Nawas laid his left hand on Patel's bed and continued.

"He means a lot to you I see"

The President looked at Nawas with surprise on his face.

"Yes he does"

Behind Nawas, Joe Sinclair opened the message in his inbox and read:

GW hospital likely to be a trap. Sending Neil Burke to coordinate getting VJ over

to Andrew's. Keep POTUS and other Principals away!!! Will advise when I know more. GC

Sinclair looked with confusion first at his pager and then at the situation unfolding in front of him. The color drained from his face as the realization hit home that it would happen on his watch.

"Then you can see him in Hell!" screamed Nawas.

In one motion he reached under Patel's sedated body, withdrew a large hypodermic needle and syringe then lunged at the President. The syringe was loaded with a mixture of potassium to stop the heart and succinylcholine to stop the breathing. Wielding the syringe like a dagger in his right hand he struck swiftly with a downward chopping motion. The needle pierced the Presidents jacket and entered the skin just above his clavicle. Nawas slammed the plunger down with his thumb and delivered the lethal cocktail then violently yanked the needle out of the Presidents chest. The President staggered away.

Pink frothy blood bubbled up from between Wallace's fingers. Nawas then turned his attention to Patel.

Agent Sinclair was the first to react but Nawas had moved with astonishing speed. Sinclair grabbed Nawas at the waist as he was turning back toward Patel's bed. Nawas braced himself by grabbing onto the railing of the bed with his left hand and with Sinclair trying to pull him away, again swung his right hand in an arc. The thick fourteen-gauge needle came down with tremendous force and entered Patels chest through his left nipple. The force of the blow then carried it through the cartilage and into Patel's heart, slicing open his left ventricle.

By now the other two agents were already hustling the stricken President out of the room. Nawas held onto the needle but now allowed himself to be dragged downward by Sinclair. This carved an arc into the ventricle and splayed it open. Nawas knowing his work was now done went limp and let himself to be subdued. He closed his eyes and mouthed a prayer. He had redeemed himself and his family.

Outside in the hallway the President clutched his chest, his heart was starting to fibrillate and the beginnings of a massive myocardial infarction were setting it. The other agents were on their radios screaming for help. They laid the President down onto a stretcher and ran it down the hallway. Nawas knew however there would be no recovery, the dose given had been massive and lethal.

Chapter 18

Andrews Air force Base is a huge sprawling facility. It is spread out over 300 acres of gently rolling hills in suburban Virginia. The base is home to the offices of several three and four star Generals as well as the barracks of a large cadre of junior enlisted airmen. From the outside however the buildings are indecipherable. The Air-force architects were instructed that from the air, a command center was to look exactly the same as a commissary, which was to look exactly the same as junior enlisted housing. From a security standpoint it made sense but from the standpoint of a visitor to the base it was like being in a hall of mirrors.

Marwan Barghouti was technically not a visitor to the base but he was just as lost. The afternoon sunlight was blinding and disorienting. He was still somewhat unsteady on his feet, his legs and arms felt heavy and his vision swam in and out of focus but he was getting stronger. With each breath he got a little better and some clarity returned to his thinking. Cyanide is a remarkably effective poison. Onset of action is almost instantaneous and death is inevitable within a minute of ingestion. Unless you have an antidote. As quick and efficient as cyanide is as a killer, its antidote is even more efficient at reversing the drug. Sodium Thiosulphate uncouples the bond that cyanide makes with oxygen and allows the poisoned blood to carry oxygen once again. Marwan Barghouti owed his life to this little wonder of pharmaceutical engineering.

Carrying the antidote had been an obvious precaution to take given the potential catastrophic consequences of an inadvertent pill rupture. When he snorted the cyanide pill in the interrogation room, the antidote tablet had popped into his mouth at the same time. He had bitten down hard into the larger pill, determined to end his life then and there. As he lay dying on the floor, gasping for air and feeling the life quickly drain out of his body, his canny survival instinct that kept him alive all these years kicked in big time. Burke and the MP's were fleeing the room in a panic, fearful for their own lives. As those final seconds of his life were counting down, the fire that makes a true fighter get up one last time to answer the bell when most people would have slipped weakly into oblivion, roared to life. He saw with sudden clarity a chance to escape, a chance for freedom and a chance to complete his mission. Using the last of his strength he forced himself to swallow the antidote and then everything had gone black.

The darkness was complete and it was alive. He was drowning in a thick black lake of oil. He struggled and kicked to get to the surface but the blackness pulled him back, embracing and enveloping him. He opened his mouth in desperation and sucked in huge lung-fulls of the blackness but instead of suffocating him, the blackness rushed in and gave him life. He had come to sitting bolt upright, gasping for air and covered in vomit. His breathing was labored, but he was alive and more importantly, the room was empty. Having pulled of coming back from the dead, the rest should be relatively easy.

His first order of business would be to blend in. He stripped to the waist and wiped his face clean of vomit and mucous and walked out into the hallway. He looked left and saw a long corridor with four doors on the left and right side. He approached the first one, put his ear to the door and heard a muffled voice on the other side. On the wall next to him was a red fire alarm lever covered with a clear plastic shield. He lifted the shield and flipped the lever into the upright position. Instantaneously a loud whooping klaxon filled the air. In the narrow corridor the sound was deafening. He burst through the door, just as a startled young man in BDU's was getting up from his desk.

Marwan screamed "Fire!, the whole building's on fire"

Confusion and fear filled the young Airman's eyes. Marwan took two steps toward him and before the airman could react, he jabbed him in the nose and then delivered a fierce flat handed slap across the larynx shattering it. Marwan then quickly lowered him to the floor keeping his mouth and nose covered until death came. He stripped the body and then hid it behind the desk, The BDU's and boots were not an exact fit and the beard was certainly a give away but it would buy him a few moments and generally that was more than he needed. He had then kept his head low and joined the crowd that was streaming out of the building. He walked right past the MP's who had been guarding him. They were still shaken from the cyanide gas and paid him no attention. I was only later, when they went back into the interrogation room to retrieve his body, that they realized that he had escaped.

Chapter 19

An unmarked black Crown Victoria sat inconspicuously outside the red brick townhouse that Janet had been moved to. Since being placed into protective custody two days ago she had been allowed to go back to her apartment in Chicago, pack and then had driven her in a two car convoy down to the safehouse in Baltimore. It was a thoroughly unremarkable building. Comfortable and anonymous. She was allowed to make one phone call a day, using the secure line within the house itself. Cell phones were deemed too risky as their location could be triangulated and tracked with the right technology but she still had hers with her just in case. While somewhat irked at the idea of having to miss work and being uprooted from Chicago Janet was trying to look at the upside. From a career standpoint she was still at the heart of one of the biggest news stories of the year and News One would be silly not to exploit it and upgrade her from weather to anchor. Also on a personal level she was grateful for the added protection from this Barghouti character. It didn't seem that his agenda would include targeting her individually but after seeing what he was capable of, the extra security was nice until Neil and Clarke finally caught this guy.

Janet was finishing up a workout when the news began to break of the days events.. She got up from doing a set of pushups and stared at the TV. On the screen the News One anchor she recognized as the normally high-strung Bill Peterson was looking decidedly somber. Janet got up and turned up the volume.

"Folks we are getting word of some events that are happening right now in our nations capital. We can now confirm that VJ Patel, the Secretary of Defense, has been shot by an lone gunman. It appears that the gunman was captured at the scene and is now in custody. Our sources tell us it is none other than Marwan Barghouti the Syrian terrorist who claimed responsibility for the horrific bombing in Chicago four days ago. "

Secretary Patel was rushed into surgery at George Washington Hospital and we have been told that he made it through surgery. But folks, this is where the story takes a turn for the worse. It appears that while President Wallace was visiting Secretary Patel he was assaulted by a trauma surgeon and sustained fatal wounds at the scene. He was pronounced dead at 5:50pm Washington time."

Peterson paused at this time, looked up at the cameras and allowed the gravity of what he had just said to sink in.

"It appears that the assassin then was also able to inflict a fatal wound to Secretary Patel before he was subdued by Secret Service Agents. At this time it is not clear how such a massive breach of security occurred but surely this is one of the darkest days in American History. There has been a massive decapitation strike launched against our country's leadership. Whether this has now been contained or is still ongoing is unclear. We have reports that the Vice-President has taken to the air and that the Speaker of the house has been sequestered to preserve the constitutional chain of command. Once again folks Andrew Wallace, the 49th President of the United states has just been assassinated."

Janet stood in shock in front of the television absorbing what she had just heard. It seemed unbelievable to her that Neil had failed, but that was exactly happened. He had been unable to stop the plot from evolving and now their President was dead. Her first instinct was to call him, maybe try to console him, tell him it would be okay. She barely knew him, in fact they had known each other for only two days but something about him made her feel safe. He was not that big or intimidating but he carried himself with an absolute confidence that she had only seen thus far in herself. He emanated an aura of competence and energy that was as appealing as it was comforting. She hesitated for a second and then got up and dialed his pager number.

4:35 pm Andrews AFB

Neil was still on the phone with Gerald Clark when his pager went off. He looked down and quickly read the text message.

Give me a call I know you must be busy but I need to talk. Janet

He made a mental note to himself to call her back when he got a moment but considering how things were going it was going to be a while.

" I can't think of what we could have done differently Neil" said Clark,

"I know you're going to beat yourself up over this one but you know as well as I do that we could not have ordered a code grey with what we had. The Secret Service would have laughed at us. We didn't have the credible evidence to suggest that he was going to go after the President and the Cabinet."

Neil stood stone faced unsmiling.

"This one's not going to get pinned on us " said Clark. "Sinclair and his boys had no right letting the President leave during a code grey. That was the breach that got him killed"

"This can't be allowed to stand Gerald. We lost a President, a cabinet member, a couple hundred civilians and this guy is still on the loose. We had him and now he's gone again. Its not just Barghouti. Someone backed him, provided material and logistical support. Someone coordinated the state side events with killing Sistani and Buchanan in Iraq."

"I know Neil, I know. The vice-president is a real dove but I can guarantee you that once Frank Beamer and the rest of Congress is done with him that he'll realize our response will have to send a clear message. I guess the only question is how are we going to go about doing it?"

"What do you mean?" asked Neil

"Well are we going to go in guns blazing like we did in Iraq and Colombia or are we going to send in some Delta force guys late at night and let them settle the score? Personally I'd go for the late night option. They'll know we're coming for them so let them sit and sweat it out."

Neil grunted in agreement. "I know a lot of guys are going to want to come out from behind the desk and saddle up for that mission."

"Neil what I can't understand though is how Barghouti got away. You said yourself you saw him drop like a rock after he swallowed that tablet."

"He must have had an antidote with him. It's the only way he could have done it. I've seen cyanide poisonings before and the smell is unmistakable. Hangs around for ever. He probably bit into the cyanide pill first to get us to unshackle him and give him first aid. Then he bit the antidote pill and hoped for the best."

"That's a hell of a gamble he took"

"You think so." asked Neil

"What do you mean?"

"Well look at it from his standpoint. If his gamble works then he's got a chance at freedom and if it doesn't then he's off to play with seventy celestial virgins for eternity. It's a win-win scenario for him"

"What are you going to do now"

"Well we've got a perimeter set up two miles out from where we last saw him. The entire base is on lockdown and we're bringing in sniper and scout army teams to track him. If we can contain him here at Andrews, then we've got him."

"Well keep me posted I've got to go now. We're having a debriefing with the VP as soon as he is sworn in."

Marwan had been in this position before. He was just as comfortable being the hunter or as in this case being the hunted. Each and every time he had been able to escape by staying calm and outthinking his potential captors. This would be no different, think three steps ahead and then act decisively. By now they must have figured out that he had escaped. They knew he was on foot and in unfamiliar territory so they would probably set up a perimeter, then they would search every square inch within that circle until they flushed him out. The homeland security agent Burke surely would lead the efforts as he would no doubt feel responsible. Marwan paused for a second to ponder this and then, mind made up, he turned around and headed back. He walked back along through the shadows to the rear of what appeared to be a storage building and then stepped out into the open. There in front of him was a small green and on the other side of it was the interrogation building he had been in a few moments ago. Four camouflaged MPRT trucks were pulling away in a cloud of dust and a few soldiers and MP's scrambled to hop in. Marwan guessed they were on their way to set up and seal the perimeter. There was a solitary panel truck left behind labeled HAZ-MAT in large red lettering across its side. He could see two workers in full yellow protective gear with hoods and respirators preparing to go inside. They checked each other's suits thoroughly for leaks and then stepped inside to begin testing the air. Marwan smiled and quickly jogged across the green and silently entered the building behind them.

Five minutes later he was zipping up his new hood and settling into the drivers seat of the HAZ-MAT truck. He fired up the engine and rumbled down the road heading west into the sun. The radio was tuned to a local shock jock on the AM band.

"This is exactly the scenario where we should nuke those bastards back to the stone-age" screamed the DJ.

"They have messed with us once too often now. Its time to

lay down the hammer and stamp out these cockroaches once and for all. You know, if we just flat out smoked the middle-east, I'd say good riddance and problem solved. Our government or what's left of it has got to get its ass in gear and exact some revenge. You know the saying that revenge is a dish best served cold? Well to hell with that! They killed our President and I say an eye for an eye, a tooth for a tooth!"

Marwan who had been more focused on navigating toward the gates, now sat straight up and stared intently at the radio. His eyes widened and slowly, disbelief turned to understanding and joy. Their mission had been a success. Nawas had succeeded after all. Burke had bluffed him. How else could he explain it? If his shot had killed Patel then there would have no reason for President Wallace to try to visit him in the hospital. The plan would have failed. Success had been predicated on Patel getting a non-lethal injury which would prompt his long-time friend Wallace to come and visit. A feeling of euphoria filled him.

All of the years of planning had come together in one of the most spectacular operations in modern history. He closed his eyes and said a silent prayer of thanks. He slowed down at a stop sign and in the distance, further down the road saw two things. The main gate about a half-mile away and about a hundred yards ahead a check-point manned by four MP's. He put the truck in gear and continued driving slowly toward the gate. His first order of business would be to wrap up a few loose ends and then terminate the mission. From the start he had realized this would be his last hurrah, there would be no returning home once he was done. He was only a few yards away from the Roadblock now. There were three large saw-horses across the road and two MP's with their M-16's slung across ambled over toward his panel truck. The Americans would hunt him down wherever he went and he would only be a liability in the future. His usefulness to Hezbollah would be counter-balanced by all of the security precautions they would have to take to keep him alive. That would only compromise the organization as a whole and decrease its effectiveness. The cyanide tablet would have been used anyway, he was under no delusions that he was a dead man walking. The only question was could he make them pay one more time before his time was up. He rolled down the window and waited for the MP's to approach.

"Hi guys see anything yet" asked Barghouti. His voice was muffled but audible from the hood.

"Nothing so far. Where's your partner?" asked the MP, looking over the van with casual indifference.

"He's still back there working but we forgot to bring the XC-46 unit. I packed the XC-31 but that's not rated for humidity greater than 75%. So either we use the XC-31 and only clear the 65 micron particles or I can go back and get the XC-46 and clear the whole building right away."

The MP whose eyes had glazed over after the first few seconds of nonsense jargon that Barghouti spouted, waved him by and looked relieved to see him go. Barghouti drove slowly and carefully to the gate where he was again waved through.

5:08 pm Andrews AFB

Neil stood silently in the back of the command post that had been set up at the MP headquarters. Technically Neil was not in charge here at Andrews. Barghouti had been handed over to military police when he was arrested and was to be treated as an illegal combatant. As such he was the property of the Department of Defense unless he managed to get off base. If he got off base and became a fugitive then the FBI and the Department of Homeland Security could legally become involved again but the commanding officer was going out of his way to extend every courtesy to Neil. Around him the office bustled with activity. He was getting updates every five min-

utes from the troops manning the perimeter. A squadron of
Rangers had just landed and would be in the field conducing a
search within five minutes, but so far all the reports had been
the same. It was almost as if he had disappeared onto thin air.
With each passing minute and no sign of Barghouti he knew
the chances for recapturing him were slipping away. Their best
chance was to contain him within the base and then flush him
out. Barghouti had allowed himself to be captured the first time
but it seemed unlikely he would allow it to happen a second
time. Neil closed his eyes and contemplated what he would do
if he were in Barghouti's shoes. The escape attempt was likely
triggered by the mistaken belief that his mission had failed. He
would initially lay low, regroup and then plan another attack.
He would eventually find out, probably within a day or two
that this would be unnecessary and then Barghouti would try
to leave the country. The safest way would be through the po-
rous border with Mexico and with a good disguise and travel
documents he could be on a plane to the Middle East in a
week. It had now been three hours since they had last seen
Barghouti and Neil's gut was telling him that it was too late.
He pounded his fist on the wall in frustration, startling the
man behind him.

"You okay sir"

"I'm fine. Its just that much more painful to actually have
him in our hands and then let him get away. Three hours ago
he was sitting in chains just two feet away from me and now,
he's vanished!"

Neil stalked away and pulled out his phone. He looked at
the text message from Janet and realized that she would have
to stay in protective custody a while longer. She was just forty-
five minutes away in Baltimore. As it stood right now, he was
just getting more and more frustrated, he needed a change and
Janet's company would be a welcome break.

He punched in her number and thumbed out a text message to her.

"I'll be over there in an hour. Lets grab some coffee and talk. Barghouti's escaped"

Neil walked over to the Colonel Chambers the CO of the MP's at Andrews.

"Colonel Chambers, I'm going to take a quick break and head over to Baltimore for a few hours. I have a witness up there I need to talk to again plus I need to clear my head. Could I bother you to let me use one of your cars?"

Chambers looked up and nodded.

"Not a problem Burke. We'll do what we can here and keep you in the loop. Here's my keys it's the white Impala right outside the door. I'm not going anywhere anytime soon, so I'll see you when you get back"

Neil thanked him, took the keys and headed out the door. The weather had turned again and in the distance Neil could see storm clouds headed in toward the city. Even though it was still relatively cool, the air felt dense and when he reached for the car door a small spark of electricity leaped form his fingers with a crack. The Impala was large, roomy and quiet. He put the car in drive and headed out toward the gate. He would take the 495 loop North and then get onto the Washington-Baltimore Parkway. At this time of day what was only a 35 mile drive would likely take a full hour. No matter, it would give him time to think and analyze the problem. He showed his ID to the gate guard and then turned right onto 337, and within a few minutes was traveling north toward Baltimore. The first few drops of rain came down slowly, hesitantly at first and then with more confidence as the sky opened up. Neil switched on the wipers and then the headlights as the afternoon light dimmed and sputtered behind the clouds. Traffic was now barely creeping along as drivers got accustomed to the abrupt gloom and adjusted to the suddenly slickened road. A few cars back and one lane over a green Mercedes sedan kept pace with Neil and when the cars slowed to merge onto the

WB parkway the Mercedes hung back a little, careful to stay within sight but never getting too close.

Chapter 20

Janet looked at herself in the mirror and decided to go with what she was wearing. It was a tight blue long sleeved shirt that clung to her like a second skin. The shirt hugged her torso and her abs were clearly visible under the material. She threw on a more sedate navy blue jacket over the shirt and looked appreciatively at her tight white cotton slacks. With the jacket on, she looked relatively conservative but if during the course of the evening she had the occasion to remove the jacket, the effect would be spectacular. With one last spritz of her Tommy Girl she was ready to go. She reached for her phone and sent Neil a quick text.

"Call me when you get outside, I'll meet you downstairs."

She then ran downstairs unlocked the front door and opened the outer screen door, the rain was really coming down now and the wind was picking up a little. In the distance she could hear the low rumble of thunder. She waved to the unmarked car that was parked outside and gestured for the policeman to come in. The patrolman got out, opened up a huge black umbrella and ran up the sidewalk. The rain splattered in through the open door and splashed onto her face as he stepped inside. His eyes opened wide as he took in her outfit.

"Everything ok ma"am" he asked.

"Oh yeah everything's fine. I just want to let you know that Neil Burke from Homeland Security is on his way over here. We're going to go out for a while so I don't want you to think I'm being abducted or anything"

The patrolman raised his eyes quizzically for a second and then nodded.

"Thanks for letting me know ma'am. I'll hang around until

Agent Burke gets here and then I'll take a little break myself and come back in an hour or so."

Janet's phone buzzed with an incoming message and she closed the door behind the policeman.

"Traffic's awful. Be there in 20 minutes. Sorry I'm late"

No problem she thought, as long as you get here Neil we're fine.

Twenty minutes later the green Mercedes was still un-obtrusively trailing Neil as he pulled up and double parked alongside the Crown Vic parked outside Janet's townhouse. The owner of the Mercedes was an accountant who had stopped at a convenience store to pick up some tissues and cold medicines. When she returned to her car there was a large panel truck parked beside it and now her unfortunate body was on the floor in the back, rolling around and bumping into the seats as Marwan went over potholes. After getting a hold of his new ride, he had sat outside of the main gate yards for 2 hours until he finally spotted Neil driving away in an Impala. He trailed Neil for the past hour unsure of how best to act but when he saw Janet running through the rain to get into the car, he smiled to himself. It would seem that Mr. Burke and the woman reporter had taking a liking to each other. Maybe they had been brought together by the stress of the moment; actually it was quite touching. It was going to be a perfect ending.

Neil opened the door for Janet and the wind, which had been dying down gusted and blew in a healthy portion of the rain storm. The thunder and flashes of lightning were becoming more frequent now and for a moment Neil wondered if they shouldn't stay inside but then he figured Janet must be getting cabin fever by now. It would be a nice change for her to get out and get some coffee.

"Hi Ms Kilpatrick, good to see you."

"Its good to see you too Neil and I thought I told you to call me Janet."

She smiled and leaned across to the drivers' side and gave him a quick hug. Neil put the car in gear and headed down the street.

"Thanks for coming up here in this weather. It's horrible"

"Yeah it just started on the way up, but really I needed to get away from Andrews and do some thinking"

"I'm so sorry Neil about what happened today. I know how hard you guys were working to catch this guy and stop his plans and now he's escaped....." she trailed off to let him fill in the details that he could.

Neil's eyes hardened.

"Janet all of this is still confidential. If we can catch him quickly we're not going to go public that he escaped. Doesn't exactly fill the public with confidence. All I can say is that he is good. We had him one moment, and the next, he was gone. We're trying to pin him down on the base but I doubt we'll be that lucky."

"Where do think he's headed?"

"If it were me I'd head down to Arizona, cross the border on foot and then try to head back to Syria." We'll set up extra security at the border the next couple of days, but I think our next real chance to get him will be when he boards a flight out of Mexico. We're going to have his picture available to all of their customs people in Mexico City and we might just pull it off that way."

They drove in silence together for the next few minutes. Neil could still smell Janet's perfume from their brief embrace and was happy to just be with her. His mood, despite the extreme circumstances was lifting. It was obvious to him that their relationship was changing but at the same time she was still a witness in a Federal case that he was in charge of. There was no way that he could take his feelings any further without seriously compromising his professionalism but at the same time he knew that he would live to regret it if he walked away from her without giving their relationship a chance to grow.

"Where do you want to go" asked Janet, interrupting his thoughts.

"I thought we'd head down to the Inner Harbor and get some coffee there. There's a Starbucks there right on the waterfront with some great views of the city."

"Sounds good to me"

They chatted pleasantly for the next few minutes as Neil navigated down from the North of the city toward the inner harbor. Janet told him about her job as a TV anchor and tried to convince him it was not as glamorous as he thought it was. Neil gave a brief commentary about Baltimore and its layout. He had been posted there for a few years early on in his career and had fond memories of biking and fishing in the city parks. For a few years in the early 90's Baltimore had briefly flirted with New Orleans as the murder capital of the US. Gun crime in the city, and especially the North Eastern and Central wards was rampant but a new mayor had taken over, brought in an outside police chief and cleaned up the city. Crime plummeted, businesses re-opened and developers had spruced up the harbor front area and made it into a major tourist attraction. Baltimore's inner Harbor was located in the upper recesses of the massive Chesapeake Bay that stretched from New Jersey all the way down to Virginia. The bay wound its way up along the eastern seaboard and finally petered out right in downtown Baltimore. The city was set out roughly in a circle with the inner harbor as its center. Neil took the Jones Falls Expressway, which ran north to south and was the major artery that linked the downtown are with the northern suburbs. On his left a green Mercedes cruised by as a gap in the traffic opened up.

"This traffic is really awful Janet, but we're almost there. I'll take the next exit and then we can park and walk a few blocks."

Don't worry about it Neil, I'm just glad to get out of that house. A girl can only work out for so many hours a day"

Without warning the grey minivan in front of them suddenly slowed and with a loud crunch slammed into the car ahead of it. Neil gripped the steering wheel tightly and glanced at his mirrors, he was boxed in by traffic on either side. No choice but to hit the brakes.

"Hold on Janet!"

He pumped the brakes hoping to bring the car to a stop, but the slick roads and the weight of the Impala caused it to fishtail, hydroplane and they struck the minivan broadside. They came to rest sideways in the road with the front of the car facing into the left lane. Neil looked up just in time to see an SUV bearing down on them on Janet's side.

"Watch out Janet" he yelled. But Janet had already tucked her head down and brought her arms up to protect herself. The SUV, a Chevy Tahoe struck them at 25 mph just behind Janet's door shattering the glass and showering them with shards. The Tahoe's airbags immediately inflated and for the next several second there was a series of crunches and thumps as a chain reaction of crashes followed. The silence that followed was peculiar and prolonged.

Janet sat in her seat for a few moments her head was swimming and her ears were ringing from the impact

"Are you okay Neil". There was no reply.

She brushed away the slivers of glass in her hair and gingerly rubbed the side of her neck. She looked over at Neil and saw that he was slumped over in his seat and moaning. His seatbelt had saved him from being ejected but the impact of the Tahoe had slammed his head into the drivers' side window shattering it and leaving him stunned.

Janet quickly released her seatbelt and leaned over to Neil. The rain was pouring in from his side and she could see a pool of blood and rain-water collecting on the floor.

"Neil! Neil! Talk to me. Are you okay!" There was no reply.

Neil moaned softly but didn't say anything. His eyes fluttered but remained closed. Janet felt the first bright flare of panic starting to swell in her chest. She opened up her door and got out into the deluge. The storm was going full blast now and in the few seconds it took to get out of the car and run around to the drivers side she was soaked to the bone. She looked through the smashed window and saw a large gash on the left side of Neil's head. It was bleeding furiously and occasionally a bright red jet of blood would spurt out and splatter against the window. She grabbed the handle of the door and tried to open it. He was losing blood every second and needed to get to a hospital but at the least she could bandage his head and stop the bleeding.

"Do you guys need any help?" a voice called out from in front of her.

Janet continued working on the car door trying to open it up.

"Yes! Yes. He's banged his head pretty badly and the doors stuck. If you have a phone can you call 911"

"I could if you'd like but I think it would just be easier to put him out of his misery now"

Janet froze and looked up. Standing three feet away, wearing green army fatigues was Marwan Barghouti.

"Did you like my little accident? That's the nice thing about German cars…they are so big and safe, I always drive one of possible. It looks like your friend Agent Burke would probably agree"

"You little fucker!" screamed Janet.

She took a quick side step to close the distance and brought her right arm up and swung a back fist at his head. Barghouti was expecting it however and caught her arm and pulled her forward and down. As she stumbled toward him he drove his knee up and delivered a crunching blow to her ribcage sending her flying back into the car door. She slid down to the ground helplessly.

"Didn't you learn from the last time we met my dear. I can see you have some training but it gives you confidence that is not yet deserved. The Israeli's teach you to fight dirty but I fight even dirtier."

"What do you want with us" she gasped. ""You've done everything you possible could"

"I'm just tying up loose ends. Your Agent Burke played a rather nasty trick on me and I intend to make him pay. You will just be a bonus"

"You can't get away! Everyone can see you. The cops will be here in a minute" As Janet painfully inched herself upright her fingers closed around a large wet glass shard in the road. Her side was on fire and it felt like she had broken a couple of ribs. She could only take shallow breaths, but the more she kept Barghouti talking the longer they could stay alive.

"I'll be done in a minute or less. Look around you. Everyone else is stuck in their cars and the highway is backed up for miles now. I will stroll out of here and be long gone before anyone notices me"

With that Barghouti crossed over to where she sat, shoved her forward and crouched down behind her. He then laced his fingers around her neck and cinched then tightly around her throat. She could feel the warmth of his breath on her neck.

"Go to sleep Janet. First you and then your boyfriend"

Janet inhaled and as the blackness began to close in willed her arms to work. Her left hand swung up holding the six-inch long shard, in what she felt was like slow motion. Her fingers were bleeding from gripping it so tightly. She aimed for his throat, but Barghouti's chin was tucked in, so the glass sliced into his right eyeball instead with a loud popping sound. The effect was instantaneous. He grabbed for his face blindly, roaring in pain and stumbled along the length of the car finally collapsing against the rear bumper.

"You bitch!" He roared.

Janet was about to answer when she heard the unmistakable sound of the hammer being pulled back on a handgun. Before she could turn two huge blasts exploded from behind her turning Barghouti's head into pulp.

"Janet I think I need an ambulance"

She turned in time to see Neil slumping toward the ground. His car door was open and he had his service revolver in his right hand. Janet caught him in time to lower him gently to the asphalt. She took off her jacket, ripped a sleeve off and used it to bandage his head.

Five days later she was back in Chicago wincing painfully around her kitchen. The rib belt that they had given her helped but the two broken ribs were going to take a while to heal. The Vice President had been sworn in as the new President and his first official order had been to mobilize the Pacific fleet to the middle-east. Syria was going to pay a heavy price.

Her phone rang, she looked at the display and smiled, it was Neil.

"Hey Janet,"

"Hello Agent Burke" she laughed and immediately grabbed her side. "How's that head of yours doing?"

"Still a little sore but I'm hanging in there. We never did get that cup of coffee Janet, so I wanted to know if you're still up for it."

"Absolutely Neil. Anytime you're in Chicago feel free to look me up, but first you've got to hurry up and get better."

"Well I heal pretty quickly and since you saved my life I think we should get to know each other a little better"

"It was my pleasure. I have to keep you alive to decide whether or not I like you."

"Well since I'm right outside why don't you come downstairs and let me in so we can start making those decisions."

Janet let out a small scream of delight and ran over to the

window. Standing on the curb waving at her with a huge bandage on his head was Agent Neil Burke.

The End